CROSSFIRE

Big trouble was brewing along the Snake. The range was plagued with rustlers, and there was dark talk of lynch law.

The number one suspect was Lin Ballou. Because Ballou rode alone, and it seemed that too often his rides were at night—on the high mesa.

But the townspeople weren't the only ones watching Ballou. His activities were also watched by the real rustlers. He was doing a job that neither group knew about, a job that put him right in the middle of the trouble. And there was no way for him to escape the crossfire. . . .

For information on ordering any of the above titles, please turn to page 128.

THE GREATEST WESTERN WRITER OF THEM ALL

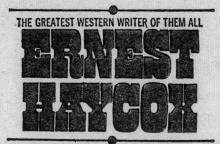

ERNEST HAYCOX

A RIDER OF THE HIGH MESA

PAPERBACK LIBRARY

NEW YORK

PAPERBACK LIBRARY EDITION

First Printing: May, 1972

This novel appeared originally in SHORT STORIES Magazine.

Paperback Library is a division of Coronet Communications, Inc.
Its trademark, consisting of the words "Paperback Library"
accompanied by an open book, is registered in the United States
Patent Office. *Coronet Communications, Inc., 315 Park Avenue
South, New York, N.Y. 10010.*

CHAPTER 1

WATER

Coming across the flat valley floor, Lin Ballou, riding a paint horse and leading a pack animal, struck the Snake River Road at a point where Hank Colqueen's homestead made a last forlorn stand against the vast stretch of sand and sage that swept eastward mile after mile until checked by the distant high mesa. It was scorching hot. The saddle leather stung his fingers when he ventured to touch it, and the dry thin air seemed to have come straight out of a blast furnace. Colqueen's dreary little tarpaper shack stood alone in all this desolation, with a barbed wire fence running both ways from it along the road—a fence that separated just so much dry and worthless land from a whole sea of dry and worthless land. And by the ditch side, Hank Colqueen himself was working away at a stubborn strand; a slow-moving giant of a man whose face and arms were blistered and baked to the color of a broiled steak.

Lin Ballou stopped beside the homesteader and threw one leg around the pommel, taking time to build himself a cigarette while passing the news of the day. He had to prime his throat with a little tobacco smoke before the words would issue from its parched orifice.

"Hank," he said, croaking, "when I see a man laboring in such misery I get mighty curious as to his hope of reward. Being a plumb honest man, just tell me what you figure that effort is going to bring you."

Colqueen straightened, dropped his wire-puller, and grinned. Speech came slowly to him, as did everything else. And first he must remove his hat and scratch a head as bald as an egg to stimulate thought. His blue eyes swept Lin, the road, the sky, and the distant mesa.

"Well," he replied at last, "I don't know as I can tell you what I'm working for. But a man's got to keep at it, ain't he? Can't see as I'm getting anywhere, but it keeps a man cooler to move than to lop around the house."

Lin Ballou laughed outright. "Always said you were honest. That's admitting more than these misguided settlers would."

Colqueen grew serious. "Well now, I don't know. When water comes to this land, it'll be Eden, and don't you forget it. This soil will grow anything from sugar beets to door knobs. Just needs a mite of water. When that comes—"

Lin groaned. "Oh, my God, you're like all the rest of them! Where's the water coming from? It won't rain in these parts six months on end. The Snake's too low to dam—and still you fellows keep hoping."

"It'll come some day," Colqueen said. "Government will find a way. Then we'll all be rich. Lin, you shouldn't be so doggoned pessimistic about it. You got a fine piece of ground yourself if you'd only farm it instead of traipsing off to the mesa all the time."

Ballou exhaled cigarette smoke and settled himself in the saddle. "My opinion of homesteading, if stated in a few words, would be something scandalous to hear. No, sir! What's the news?"

"Nothing much," Colqueen said, eyeing Lin's pack animal more closely. "Still prospecting?"

"Yeah."

Colqueen studied the younger man at some length

6

and finally turned toward his work. Quite as if by afterthought he threw one piece of information over his shoulder. "Been more cattle rustled this last week while you was gone. Cattlemen's Committee is about ready to do something."

"Yeah?" Lin drawled. "Cattle certainly are fickle creatures. Well, so long." He spoke to his tired horse and traveled on, the dust rising behind him.

Colqueen shot a last look at the pack animal and issued a statement to himself. "Says he's prospecting out in the high mesa—but I swear I never seen him packing pick or shovel. Kind of funny, too, when a man stops to think of it, that some of this rustling goes on while he's doing this prospecting. Guess it ain't none of my business. I sure like Lin—but he's getting a bad name for himself with all this mysterious loping around the country."

Lin Ballou kept on his way. Colqueen's shanty dwindled in the distance and finally was lost behind a solitary clump of poplars. The morning's sun grew hotter, and the mesa became but a shadow in the heat fog that shimmered over the earth. Relaxing, Lin noted occasional patches of land enclosed by fence that had been given up long ago, and homestead shacks that were vacant and about to fall apart. It took unusual persistence to stick in this country. Once it had belonged exclusively to cattlemen—free range that had no fence or habitation from one day's ride to another. Then the craze for farms had stricken the country and a wave of settlers had penetrated the valley. The sturdy and the stubborn had stayed on while the weak departed.

It was no place, Lin reflected, for a fellow who didn't have a lot of sand in his craw and a boundless store of hope in his heart. As for himself, he failed to see where the homesteader could ever prosper. The land was meant for cattle—and possibly for one other industry. He rode on, thinking about that.

The sun flamed midway in the sky when he came to his own house—which in his early enthusiasm he had built somewhat larger and better than most others in the valley—and put up his horses. He cooked himself a dinner, looked around to see what had happened during his week's absence, saddled again and set out southward toward town—especially toward Gracie Henry's home. Traversing the three-mile stretch, he kept thinking about Hank Colqueen's last statement. More cattle missing, he mused. Guess I knew that before Hank did. And from all appearances there'll be others missing shortly. He smiled somewhat grimly. Hank sure aimed that statement at me. He sure did.

The Henry house, a neat affair in white and green, showed through a group of trees, and Lin, with a quick rise of spirits, trotted into the yard and slid from the saddle, grinning widely.

"Alley-alley-ahoo! Come and see what the great snow-storm left on your porch."

A girl pushed through a screen door and waved her hand gaily.

"Welcome, dusty traveler. You've been gone longer than you said you would be."

She was a lithe, straight girl with burnished red hair and clear, regular features. In some manner the heat and the sand and the hardships had left no mark on her. She seemed as exuberant and happy as if this valley were a blossoming paradise. And she also seemed glad to find Lin Ballou before her. Lin removed his hat and rubbed the whiskers on his face ruefully.

"Shucks," he said, "I guess nobody'd care much if I never got back."

8

"Fishing, Mister Man," she retorted. "I never answer that statement, and you ought to know it by now."

"Uh-huh, I do, but a fellow can keep trying, can't he? You might make a mistake some day. And where is the Honorable Judge Robert Lewis Henry?"

"Dad's in the house." Suddenly eagerness spread over her face. "Tell me, quick, Lin, did you have any luck this time? Did you find color?"

"There's color all over the earth, ma'am. In the sky, in the grass—"

She stamped her foot. "Don't fool me. I mean your prospecting. Did you find a sign of gold?"

The humor died from him and his lean sunburned face became impassive. "Well, I think we've got a chance—"

"We? Who is 'we'?"

He caught himself. "Just a way of saying myself," he corrected.

She moved forward and caught his eye with such soberness and speculation that after a moment he looked away. Not that he was shifty-eyed. There was just something so troubled in her face, something so wistfully troubled that it troubled him.

"Lin, you always fence with me. I never know the truth. Why don't you tell me things? Especially now when everybody—" She stopped short, seeing that her tongue was about to betray her.

Lin Ballou spoke sharply. "Everybody saying what? What's folks been telling you? Meddling like they always do, I suppose. Nosing into other folk's business. Gracie girl, what have they said to you?"

"No," she replied, "I'll not repeat gossip. You'd think I believed it, and I don't. Only—"

The screen door groaned. A short, stubby man with a choleric face and white hair came to the porch and ad-

9

justed his glasses. This operation completed, he bent upon Lin a glum, severe gaze, pursing his lips first one way and then another. He had an air of self-importance, and though no more than a dirt farmer, he always wore a stiff shirt and high collar. Once upon a time he had been justice of the peace in some eastern state. On coming west he had clung to the title, and since he knew a smattering of law, the homesteaders often brought trivial legal matters to him for his advice.

"Howdy, Judge," Lin said, throwing up a friendly hand. "Hope you got wood enough to keep you warm in this winter weather."

"Hem," said the judge, as if reluctant to answer Lin. "Back from your futile occupation, I see." Sarcasm came readily in his words. "Find any fool's gold?"

"Well, to pair that question, I might ask you if you found any fool's water yet," Lin replied amiably.

Judge Henry threw back his head as if the answer had been an affront to his dignity. Presently he went on, in a still more sarcastic strain. "You may speak lightly if you choose, but water is more apt to come to us as a result of our labor than gold is to you—if indeed you go into the mesa for that particular purpose."

The intent of the last phrase was too plain to overlook. Grace put an arm on her father's shoulder as if to curb his hostility. Lin regarded him soberly.

"What might you believe I do in the mesa, Judge? Have you got some idea on the matter?"

But the judge, having launched the hint, would not develop it. "Meanwhile your land lies idle. What do you intend to do with it, young man?"

Lin had recovered his temper again. "Do as everybody else does, sir. Pray for water that will never come."

Judge Henry shook his finger at Lin. "As to that, young man, you are mistaken. We will get water." He turned

10

on his heel and retreated into the house. The screen slammed behind him. Lin smiled at Grace.

"Judge Robert Lewis Henry entertains no high opinion of me, that's mighty plain. Well, the way of true love—"

"Lin!" Grace said, and grew somewhat red. "But don't be angry at Dad. He has his own troubles."

"Yeah. I guess we all do, Gracie girl. Let me see, this is dance night, ain't it? Are you going with me, or have I lost out?"

"Going with you, Lin. Come to supper?"

He retreated to his pony. "You bet I will. Now, I've got to journey into the metropolis of Powder and stock up. Bye-bye."

Three hundred yards down the road he turned in his saddle to see her by the corral, watching him with shaded eyes. He flung up a hand and went on.

That father of yours is sure a snorter, he thought. It does seem like there's a lot of unkind words being propagated against me lately.

He would have been more certain of that if he had been able to overhear Judge Henry's remarks to Grace when she stepped back into the house. The judge stood framed in the office doorway, a pudgy, disapproving statue of righteousness.

"Daughter, did I understand you to say you would go to the dance with that Ballou vagrant?"

"Vagrant? Dad, what queer, unkind words you use."

"Hem! He's no less than that and probably a great deal more. Do you know what's being said about him, daughter? It's said that he's no less than a cattle thief, and I'll not—"

"Dad, he is no such thing!" Grace cried. "Don't you

11

spread gossip like that. It's not right. Who told you he was a thief?"

"Oh, different parties," Judge Henry answered vaguely.

"And how do those different parties know?" she persisted. "How I hate a man or woman who'll sneak around spreading gossip. Lin Ballou is as honest as daylight!"

The judge's favorite weapon was sarcasm and he fell back upon it. "So he's such a fine, upright, industrious man, eh? Seems to me you take a great deal of interest in protecting him."

"I do," Grace admitted.

"Hem," the judge muttered. "I don't want him around this place. I'm an honest man and I've got a reputation to keep."

But Grace had a mind and temper of her own. She had cooked and washed and labored and kept books many years for her father and she was not afraid of him.

"Don't you mind your reputation," she said, turning into the kitchen. "He's coming to supper, and I'm going to make him the best apple pie he's ever tasted. He looked thin."

Lin Ballou, in jest, had styled Powder a metropolis, and indeed some of the merchants of the town assiduously worked to make it such. But when Lin Ballou drove into the main street from the road, he had to admit that Powder seemed doomed to crumble into the element it was named after and float away. Once it had been a sinful, turbulent little cattle town. In a later day the homesteaders had appropriated it. Now, with the land boom a thing of mournful history, it rested somnolently and nearly bankrupt under the baking sun, its single row of buildings half tenantless, the paint peeling off. With an eventful history behind it, Powder looked forward—or at least the merchants did—to the time when

12

water should come to the valley and give it another era of prosperity.

Lin hitched his pony on the shady side of the street and walked into the post office for his mail. There was, he found, quite a stack of letters and printed matter, the latter bearing the stamp of the U.S. Geological Service. Primus Tabor, the postmaster, passed them through the wicket with a question propounded in an innnocent tone.

"Ain't seen you for a spell, Lin. Been back on the high mesa?"

"Uh-huh."

"Well, is prospecting any better than homesteading?"

There was an edge to the question, but when Lin looked up from his mail, he saw nothing but a cadaverous and foolish countenance that seemed incapable of much malice.

"About fifty-fifty," he said, and departed.

"Huh," muttered the postmaster, slamming the wicket door.

No anger like that of a born gossip foiled, Lin meditated, holding one particular envelope to the light. And to judge from all the finger marks on these here epistles, somebody's been trying to read through them. Guess I'll have to get my mail through .another channel. Won't do at all to have the news inside become common property. No, *sir*.

He was on the point of crossing the street when ho became aware of a burly figure in sombrero and riding boots stamping down the walk toward him. No second glance was needed to recognize the man; Lin saw him with a sudden quickening of pulse. Instead of crossing, he walked straight forward. Abreast of the big man, he nodded and spoke casually.

"Howdy, Mr. Offut."

The man slowed in his course, cast one glance beneath

his broad hat brim, and then without as much as a nod, swung on. Lin turned sharply, traversed the street and, with a face bereft of emotion, went into the store. It took him but a few minutes to get a gunny sack filled with provisions. Emerging, he got to his horse and soon was beyond the town, striking toward his own place by a short-cut.

Ballou had no sooner left town than Postmaster Tabor left his office and crossed over to the store. Tabor found no one in the dim interior except the owner of the place, and after a glance behind him, Tabor broke into a mysterious mumble-jumble.

"See it! See what I saw? Guess that makes it certain, don't it?"

"Huh? Grab hold of your tongue," the storekeeper advised.

"Why, damnation," the postmaster growled, "didn't you see Offut snub Lin Ballou? Passed him by with nary a word."

"Yeah, I saw it."

"Well, then, what do you think?"

"Same as you."

"Lin Ballou," the postmaster stated with gusto, "is guiltier than a licked dog. If he wasn't, why should old man Offut—he's the body and soul of the Cattlemen's Committee remember—Why should Offut treat him so cold, 'specially when he and Ballou was once the best of friends?"

"Two and two make four," the storekeeper stated. "Now he says he's prospecting all by himself. Yet he comes and buys grub enough for two-three people. What's that mean?"

"Means him and somebody else is rustling cows," the postmaster said. "And I reckon Offut and the cattlemen

14

know it. Oh, there'll be a necktie party plenty soon enough."

"Doggone," the storekeeper broke in, aggrieved. "When that happens, I'll lose a darn good account."

"I reckon lots of people hereabouts have got Lin Ballou judged right," the postmaster said. "As for all them papers from the Geology Department—that's just a bluff."

"Listen," warned the storekeeper, "don't you go talking too much. Mebbe he's rustling and mebbe folks are getting onto it, but even so, he's got a powerful lot of friends and he's a hard, hard fellow himself. So be careful."

The sun, going westward, threw its long shadows across the valley and struck the high mesa with a glow of flame. Presently, as Lin traveled, something like a breath of air fanned his cheeks, and the distant mesa turned to purple. The heat of the day vanished and then the outline of the distant crags and turrets stood out as if but a short mile or two away.

How deceptive that high mesa was, Lin mused, sweeping its bulk with an affectionate eye. The sight of it was deceptive, and over beyond, among its folds and pockets, there were other deceptions. For along its base and beyond its farther side lay the last of the cattle ranges. And a man might wander for days from point to point, never catching a clear sign of man or beast, yet all the while be within a quarter mile of some hidden bowl harboring both.

Folks might be surprised if they knew what was going on right now in those ridges, he thought, and sunk his head, grateful for the freshening breeze. Half a mile away his house stood to view, the windmill beside it catching the first puffs of wind.

Offut now—he certainly did make a fine spectacle,

Ballou told himself. I guess most of the citizens of Powder saw that little scene. Lin Ballou, spurned, scorned, rebuked in plain daylight. Marked, branded, scorched and otherwise labeled as being a cattle thief. He spoke aloud bitterly, wrinkles crowding around his eyes. There was an impotent anger in the way he struck his doubled fist against the saddle leather. "Sure. The story will be all over the country in five hours. Well, I guess I can play the game through now. Man's got to make a living somehow in this cussed country. Grace, you poor kid. You'll sure have a heart burning when you hear it."

He halted in front of his house and slid from the saddle. Throwing the sack of provisions down, he was on the point of leading the horse around to the barn when an outline in the sand caught his eye. It was the long narrow print of a cowhand's boot with the sharp heel gouging well into the earth; not a single print, but several, each leading forward and ending at the door. Lin's eye caught a small slit of light between the casing and the door itself. He had closed that door on leaving the house, and now it stood slightly ajar.

In a single move he drew his gun and kicked the portal wide, weaving aside a little to protect himself.

"Come out of there!"

A chair scraped and a voice said gruffly, "Put your thunder wagon down. Hell, can't a man take a rest without being called on it?" And directly after the voice, a strange, uncommonly ugly creature stepped up to the threshold. He was a larger man than Lin Ballou, though his frame carried more fat than Ballou's. He was older, too, with a jaw that shot out beyond the rest of his face and was covered with a metal-blue stubble. He wore black, slouchy clothes and from below his hat came a cowlick that plastered itself closely to his forehead. A toothpick hung from one side of his mouth and gold

16

teeth glittered when he spoke. A gun rested against each hip, and his eyes were themselves almost as piercing as weapons, being a kind of steely black.

"Well, well," Lin said with assumed pleasure, "if it ain't our friend Beauty Chatto. Lost your way, Beauty? Last I knew, your shanty was west about two miles."

"I come on a particular, personal visit," Beauty said. "And I been waiting for quite a spell. Took you a powerful time to negotiate the road between here and Powder and back."

"Watchin' me pretty close, Beauty?"

The steely eyes emitted a flash and the jaw closed vigorously. "Tell a man, Lin. You don't know how close I been a-watching you—me and Nig both."

"Guess it must be a professional interest," Lin murmured.

"Well," Beauty growled, abandoning the toothpick, "I'm getting tired of the watching, so I come to warn you. Make out as if you're prospecting if you want, but that ain't fooling the Chatto family. Nary a bit. A prospector don't go sashaying from hell to breakfast like you do. 'Tween day before yesterday and yesterday night you was all the way from Rooster's Pinnacle to the Punch Bowl. Prospector? Hell, no!"

"Proceed," Lin urged. "What follows?"

Chatto straightened. "This, hombre. You ain't nothing more nor less than a spy, and we ain't gonna have you cluttering the high mesa. Cut it out. Stay away. Vamoose —or get took real sick."

"Moving papers, in short," Lin summed up, watching the man through half-closed eyes. "Your business won't stand inspection, will it, Beauty?"

"Why," Chatto said frankly, "I ain't afraid to admit Nig and me is rustlers—to you, at least. Reckon lots of folks suspect it, but that ain't proof. Point is—you stay

17

away or you'll stumble on us one of these times and get killed."

"Which is bad. But you got me completely wrong, Beauty. I'm a prospector and I'll stick to it. Going into the high mesa tomorrow."

Chatto stretched his arm and stabbed Ballou with a finger. "Take warning, now! I ain't going to look for trouble. You know me. I know you. Just stay away. There's plenty of places to *prospect* aside from the high mesa."

"Going in tomorrow night," Lin announced. "Much obliged for the warning."

Chatto turned the corner of the house, dived into the barn and reappeared with his horse. From the saddle he made his last announcement. "You think that over, Lin. I ain't sore—yet. Don't like to kill a man before I give him time for studying. Think it over."

He flung his quirt at the horse's rump and rode off at a lope. Ballou put up his pony and returned to the house. Before going inside, he scanned the heavens.

Rain? he thought. Shucks, no. No water in sight. Yet I bet every blessed man inside of fifty miles is praying for it. Some of these homesteaders would kill for an inch of water. He shook his head, far from feeling the humor that he had used all day among the people of the valley.

In that gloaming hour everything seemed discouraging. Even more, there was a portent of ruin in the air. All over this parched floor men were keeping up a flame of hope that must inevitably flicker out; and as for himself, he knew that by morning his own name would be further blackened by suspicion. What was to come of all this? And what would Gracie think?

CHAPTER 2

A SECRET MEETING

At the very time Lin Ballou had ridden in and out of Powder, a secret parley of three men was going on in the back room of Lawyer Dan Rounds' office. Of all places to meet this was the strangest, for it was piled high with dusty, unclaimed trunks, bundles of law journals, and all the bric-a-brac that a man of the legal profession might collect in fifteen years of varied practice. However, these three wished no publicity on this particular occasion and had gathered as quietly as possible. Rounds had casually slipped from the front of his office to the rear and locked the intervening door. Archer Steele, cashier of the bank, had traversed the back lots and was already present. While the two debated in a subdued tone, they were joined in the same manner by the third, James J. Lestrade.

He was easily the most imposing of the group, this Lestrade; a jolly, bluff man, who wore good clothes and had a ready tongue for everyone he met. He was a cattleman, though he spent little enough time on the Double Jay, preferring to leave most of the routine to his foreman. It suited him better to have a small office adjoining that of Rounds and here he liked to play politics on a small scale. When he was not doing this, he was traveling across the country or to the stockyards at Portland—anything to give an outlet to his restless nature. Since he liked the limelight, it was therefore very strange to find him in this dusty lumber room of old relics. Characteristically, he had a joke on the tip of his tongue as he brushed the top of a trunk and gingerly sat down.

"Well, boys, you can't say I'm modest, but this time the old man doesn't want everybody hearing his big bassoon."

"Better lower your tone, then," Rounds advised dryly. "Sometimes I think you must have learned to speak amongst a bunch of bawling heifers."

"Well, Dan, the louder you talk the more people will hear you. And I like to be heard. Howsomever, we'll try to 'bide the warning. Now as to the business in hand, here's some reading material that ought to be interesting. Cast an eye over it." He drew a long yellow paper from his inner pocket, smoothed it on his knees and gave it to Rounds. The latter settled down to a slow, painstaking perusal, at which Lestrade presently grew impatient. "For God's sake, it ain't necessary to read the commas and periods. Hurry along. Get the nubbin—that's all."

Rounds finished with it and passed it to Steele, who flashed a rather careless glance across the page and folded it. "Not being scientific," he said, "I don't comprehend all the figures."

"Sum and substance is," Lestrade explained, "that the quicker we get the land in this valley tied up, the sooner we'll be millionaires."

Rounds looked behind him uneasily and again warned Lestrade to lower his voice. There was a long period of silence, broken finally by the lawyer.

"This much is certain—we're not going to get any place trying to buy land piece by piece. Sooner or later the folks would wake up and get suspicious of our purpose. Another thing, there's homesteaders who are holding on with their eyeteeth, and it would take considerable money to meet their price. Conservatively speaking, you hold mortgages on about a thousand acres and you might buy—quietly, a piece at a time—as many more without exciting comment. Why won't that satisfy?"

"No," Lestrade said, and explained himself in a single phrase. "Whole hog or none. What's two thousand acres in a deal like this? I want the whole valley—or most of it—right under my finger. Moreover, the most important location is where I'd have the hardest time buying. I mean the stretch from Colqueen's down through Henry's and clear to the edge of the town. You see it shaded on the map you've got."

"Don't see how it's to be done," Rounds stated.

Lestrade sat back, his round pink face beaming. "I do. Came to me in a flash last week. Been nursing it ever since. Even got the ball rolling. Simple as falling off a horse. We're going to bankrupt the folks in the valley. Make 'em so poor they can't pay their interest on their mortgages—seventy per cent have got their places in hock—and then take up these mortgages. The rest will be so doggoned discouraged they'll sell for a song and leave the country. See?"

"Simple," Rounds agreed, but with some amount of sarcasm. "How does a man bankrupt a hundred and fifty settlers all at once?"

Lestrade put a counter-question, leaning forward on his trunk and waggling a finger at the two. "What's the single thing folks in this country want most of all?"

"Water," Steele answered as if the word had been on the tip of his tongue.

"Right!" Lestrade boomed, forgetting himself. "And they're in a state of mind where they'll fall in with any

21

harebrained scheme to get it. Well, my scheme ain't harebrained. Up on the mesa is Lake Esprit. That's in my holdings. Well, we are going to organize a settlers' company and run a ditch into the valley from the lake. Each stockholder gets the benefit of it. The more money he puts in, the more stock he gets and the more dividends he draws when the profits begin to arrive. Then—"

"When you've got the money from them to start building the ditch," Rounds interrupted thoughtfully, "you'll skip out, I suppose, and let some dummy corporation foreclose."

"Oh, nothing as raw as that," Lestrade protested. "We'll actually start work. Make some mistake in construction so that it'll cost a lot of money and finally go busted. That won't be difficult. Make it seem like there's no fraud. But the settlers, having put their money into the scheme—and I'll lay they'll fall for it hand over head —won't have a dime to keep on with homesteading. Them that are mortgaged will sell out in order to save something from the wreck. The rest will be so plumb discouraged they'll do likewise. I've already organized a corporation, a dummy one, like you say, in Portland, and transferred the mortgages to it. Meanwhile, it'll be buying more mortgage paper off the local bank, which is pretty heavily loaded—"

"Wait a minute," Steele said. "I don't understand half of this."

Both Rounds and Lestrade looked impatiently toward the cashier. Lestrade made another effort to explain the plan, but broke off in the middle with a grunt. "Hell, it ain't necessary for you to get the workings of it. All you need to know is that we're making a move to get control of this valley. We'll do it in a legal way, what's more."

"Yes," Steele said, "but if the settlers find out we're

working crooked there'll be trouble for us. I don't fancy violence."

"No," Lestrade agreed, "you wouldn't. You like your skin. Never mind. When the storm breaks, we'll all be out of the way and let the dummy corporation and the law officers execute the rest of the plan. We'll be in Portland, directing things from there."

Rounds was surveying the plan from various angles, his busy mind bosltering it here and there with certain expedients.

"Now, first of all, you'll have to keep the money you raise in the local bank. That's for the sake of appearances. Everybody knows the bank is honest."

"Agreed," Lestrade said.

"Next, we'll have Steele here made treasurer of the fund. He'll issue money on the labor warrants and for supplies. He being also connected with the bank, he'll be above suspicion."

"Well," Lestrade chuckled, "nobody but you and I know he's crooked."

Steele's impassive countenance reddened a little. "That's a harsh word, Lestrade."

"Don't be mealy-mouthed," the big man retorted. "I never drew an honest breath and I ain't ashamed to admit it. Only folks don't know I'm crooked. So long as we three keep that information under our hats, all will be fine. Go on, Dan. Your legal mind can fix things up as they ought to be fixed."

"The most essential thing," Rounds went on, "is to have some one of the settlers promote this thing himself. They'll take it better if one of their own kind sets the ball rolling. Then you can come in as the man willing to do the organizing and directing."

Lestrade smiled again. "Already thought of the very person. "

"Who?"

"Judge Henry. He's a damn fool if there ever was one. An ounce of flattery will swell his head bigger than a balloon. But the settlers seem to think he's pretty shrewd, so he's our instrument. That's easy. I'll go out this afternoon and see him myself."

"As for organization and the legal end, I'll take care of that," Rounds resumed. "But why are you in such a hurry?"

Lestrade lost his good humor. "I got a reason to believe there's others who suspect what we've already discovered. Can't let a thing like this lag. I won't have an easy minute until the land's under my thumb."

"Who do you suspect?" Rounds demanded.

"Lin Ballou. He's doing too much prospecting to suit me. Common talk is that he's looking for gold, but if that's so, why should he be traveling back and forth on the valley floor? Any fool knows gold ain't found in such places."

Dan Rounds got up, and for the first time he showed anger. "Yes, and there's a lot of talk around here about his being a rustler. I'd like to find the gent who said as much to me! By Godfrey, I'd wring his neck. Lin Ballou's my friend. He don't know I'm crooked, but I know he's as straight as a string. Rustling talk is all nonsense. As for him being what you think—I doubt that, too. If he says he's prospecting for color, you can believe every word of it."

"All right, all right," Lestrade said. "I didn't mean to rub your fur the wrong way. But, anyhow, it don't pay to let the fat fry too long. I want to get things wound up. Meeting's adjourned. I'm going down to see Henry right off."

Rounds moved toward the door. "I'll rig up the preliminary papers. Now, as I see it, you're the only one

24

interested in this scheme, so far as folks are to understand. Steele and I are just to be instruments. Naturally you and the settlers will come to me to take care of the legal end, but they won't know our connection."

"You've got a good head," Lestrade said. He opened the back door, surveyed the lot for a moment and disappeared.

Shortly, Steele followed suit. Rounds unlocked the intervening portal and let himself back into the front office. The street was deserted. The sun blazed down, relentless in its heat. Rounds took a drink of water from the cooler and wiped the sweat away from his forehead. The meeting had not left him in any serene frame of mind, for though money and power were things he worshiped and now was on the path to gaining, he could not quite bury the uneasy voice of conscience. He strode to the door and looked up and down the dusty thoroughfare. Some distance away, Lestrade cruised slowly toward the stables, his corpulent body swaying and his loose coat flapping. A town loafer sprawled in the shade, asleep. Other than that, the place seemed abandoned, utterly dead. Rounds thought about it, bitterly.

Fifteen years I've spent hereabouts. What's it brought me? Not so much as a county judge's job. Heat and sand and trouble! Why the devil should I worry about what happens to the homesteaders? They wouldn't worry about me if I was sunk. Let 'em scrabble.

But even as he thought it, he knew he would never convince himself. Somehow, they made no men in the world like the men of this valley. There was, for instance, Lin Ballou. Why, he could trust his very life to Lin.

Yet all Lin gets is a bad name for cruising around, he thought. A lot of buzzards!

Suddenly he remembered that when this new plan was

consummated he would have to leave the valley forever and at the thought of it he retreated to his desk and sat down. The heat and the grit and all the troublous elements were a part of him. Going back over the years, he remembered the flaring feuds, the shooting scrapes, and the torrid courthouse trials. There was vitality in this land that he knew he should never find in another.

Trouble with me is, I'm not enough of a crook, he thought. Funny thing. Now, Steele, he never did have a conscience—but I think he's yellow. Lestrade's the man! He never had a conscience and he never showed far. A born crook. Well, the eggs are broken now. Got to go through with it.

A nondescript figure ambled through the door.

"Dan, I want you should fix me an affidavit," he said. "It's a personal matter—but I know you're plumb honest."

CHAPTER 3

THE CROSS-ROAD'S SCHOOL

James J. Lestrade took his time, for he had discovered long ago that a fast pace unsettled his corpulent body and soon tired any horse that carried him. He thought better, too, when giving his animal free rein; and that, despite the torrid sun and the dust creeping up his nostrils, made him in a degree oblivious to physical discomfort. He was always pulling strange schemes from the back of his head, and turning them over and over, and returning most as being too daring or too impractical. Nearly anything was grist for his mind and above all, he liked to take the various men he knew and pull them apart.

He prided himself in this. It was his own belief that he understood perfectly the foibles and vanities of the settlers; and he found a great deal of pleasure in running down the roster of friends and acquaintances and affixing to each name a certain tag. This man had a price. That man could not be bought. In the present circumstances he was inspecting those particular ones who were most vitally connected with his irrigation plan. Foremost, of course, were Dan Rounds and Archer Steele, and as he closed his heavy lids, he summoned their faces before him.

Best I could do under the situation, he thought. Howsomever, both are feeble props. Dan, he might go back on me. I can see that right plain. Got to get him involved so he can't. When the time arrives that I can do without his help, I'll find a way to throw him over. As for Steele, it's plumb necessary to watch him close. That man's a snake. He'd do me in in a minute if he had the nerve. Got to watch him. Now, let's see what we're going to tell Judge Henry.

By the time he reached the Henry place he had smoothed every wrinkle of his plan, making note of little points here and there that would appeal to the Judge's inordinate vanity. And when he tied his horse to the corral and mounted the porch he summoned all his affability and humor. The judge, he found, was rocking himself on the porch, half shrouded in the settling dusk.

"Howdy, Judge Henry," he said, stressing the title. "You see a weary man before you that's traveled a mighty hot road just to make a particular call. Hope you bear this heat better than I do."

The judge, instantly flattered by the visit, pursed his lips and motioned to an adjoining chair. "Hem. Sit down. Not going any farther tonight, are you? Well, you'll have supper with us. A particular visit, you say?"

"Let's go into your office," Lestrade suggested.

Judge Henry rose with alacrity. At the screen door Lestrade met Grace and drew off his hat, all smiles. "Miss Grace, your dad asked me to supper and I sure hope you'll second the motion."

"Good evening, sir. We'll be mighty glad to have you, providing you won't mind the cooking."

Lestrade looked down at the red hair, shimmering now under the hall light. His heavy lids drooped. "Grace, I'd feel honored to eat it the rest of my born days. Judge, your girl's getting pretty enough to steal. You want to watch out."

"Well," the judge said, "there's some that I got an eye on. A man that's an ordinary vagrant can't marry my daughter."

Lestrade's body shook with a kind of internal laughter. He touched Grace's shoulder with a finger, but at the sight of her eyes, he suddenly drew the finger away.

"Guess I better not be so shiftless then. Might want to throw my hat in the ring if I thought there was a chance."

The two men passed down the hall, and presently shut themselves in the judge's office. Grace stood silent, her face turned toward the door. She had come out of the kitchen at the first sound of the visitor, thinking it was Lin Ballou. Lestrade had received her welcoming smile quite under false pretenses, for it certainly had not been meant for him.

What does he want with my father? she asked herself,

28

the worry creeping into her forehead. What would any cattleman want from a homesteader? He may flatter poor Dad, but I see through that fine talk. And he'd better keep his fat old hands away from me.

There was a whistle from the corral. She went eagerly through the screen to meet Lin.

"Hope I ain't late," he apologized, "but I had to do a little currying and brushing. Fellow like me is under an awful handicap. Nature did such a blame poor job that it takes a lot of bear oil and harness grease to piece out. Anyhow, I guess you can recognize me."

"Lin," she said plaintively, "I wish you wouldn't always low-grade yourself. Why, I think you're good looking—"

"Now, Gracie, you be careful. You're a lot too young to start in on perjury."

"Lin, you come out to the kitchen with me while I dish up. Dad, he's got company. Mr. Lestrade came on some errand and they're in the office. I know I shouldn't be fussing about such things, but this worries me. Why should a cattleman have business with a homesteader?"

She looked up to see his expression. Lin was staring down the hall.

"Can't tell," he replied. "Lestrade's got an iron in 'most every fire."

Her fingers went up to a button of his coat. "You're thinking something else," she said. "Whenever you assume that poker face, I know there's solemn thoughts behind it. But what if he has got an iron in every fire? There's no fire here."

"Yes, there is. Gracie, you're the fire."

"Lin, how you talk! Mr. Lestrade wouldn't spend any time on me."

"No?" Lin said. "He'd be crazy if he didn't."

"Hush." She led him into the kitchen and ordered him

29

around so fast he had little time to talk. But when the pie came out of the pantry and was placed on the table, he grinned from ear to ear.

"Gal, you know how to flatter a man's stomach. I've got a notion—"

The notion, whatever its nature, was interrupted. The office door opened and the judge, followed by Lestrade, came into the dining room. The judge had a glum, owlish look for Lin which the young man answered with a cheerful grin. Lestrade spoke jovially to him, though he passed one swift appraising glance to the girl first.

"Howdy, Lin, howdy. Ain't seen you for a small coon's age. What keeps you away from the town these days?"

"Prospecting," the judge said ironically. "Sit down, Mr. Lestrade, and eat. Pass the meat ad gravy, Gracie. Hem. Guess you never believed me when I said we'd get water some day, did you, young man? Well, I'm old enough, I hope, to know better. We're going to have water in this valley and we're going to have it soon. How's that sound to your intelligence?"

The man was inflated with importance. He pursed his lips in all manner of shapes, his shoulders thrown back and his pudgy body as straight as a ramrod. Lestrade beamed at him, which caused Lin to make a thoughtful reservation.

"Of course there was an iron in the fire," he said to himself. "Maybe two of 'em." Aloud he asked, "Where's this water coming from, up or down?"

"It's coming," the judge announced, "from Lake Esprit, and it'll be brought by a main ditch right into the valley. Mr. Lestrade and I have come to several important conclusions which the settlers will agree with as soon as I call a meeting. If you should like to know more —though from the foolishness in your head I'm not sure you would—I might say it will be a cooperative concern, headed by myself and Mr. Lestrade."

"Oh," Lin said, and for a moment he forgot the company and the food. His mind raced back and forth, all the while filling with suspicion. "Who's to supply the money?"

"The stockholders. In other words, the settlers."

Lin pushed his plate back and spoke with a sudden vehemence that surprised them all. "You mean to tell me you're rushing into a private irrigation system when none of you knows beans about it? How much money do you think this valley holds, anyhow? It will cost a pile and don't you forget it. Mr. Lestrade, if this is your suggestion, I sure don't think much of it."

Lestrade was annoyed and showed it. But a lifelong training in suavity came to his rescue. "You understand, of course, that as soon as news of the project gets abroad, the whole valley will fill with prospective landowners and they'll take up their part of the burden."

"Maybe they will, and maybe they won't," Lin said. "Seems like there's a lot of guesswork in that. And when you build water ditches you don't want to do any guessing."

"As for that," Lestrade said, "I've already had an engineer estimate the cost. I'm afraid, Lin, that you're a little shortsighted on this water situation. I think the settlers have more faith than you've got."

"That's the point," Lin said. "They've got water on the brain and they'll rush into all sorts of foolish things."

"Let them judge whether it's foolish or not," Judge Henry shouted. His pride had been sadly punctured by Ballou's questioning of his judgment and he viewed the young man with increased dislike.

"They can judge all they please," Lin said, "but not

before I've done a little campaigning myself. I don't like the notion and I'll tell them why."

"Why should you concern yourself?" Lestrade said sharply.

Lin looked the big man directly in the face. "Mr. Lestrade, I was born and raised hereabouts and I've seen a heap of suffering from this dry-land farming. Maybe I'm a fool, but I can't stand by and see all these folks rush into crazy ideas. They're my kind of people, that's why."

Gracie, who had been listening with troubled eyes, broke in. "No more, you folks. I'll not have my supper spoiled this way. Stop your arguing."

And so the meal ended in a truce. The men retired to the porch while Gracie prepared for the dance. Judge Henry became so interested in his talk with Lestrade that he forgot about hitching up and had to be sent to the job by his daughter after she was ready.

The Saturday night dance at the cross-roads school was almost the only recreation the valley had and consequently it was the gathering point for all those within forty miles. The younger ones, like Lin and Gracie, came to enjoy themselves, while the older men and women sat around the wall and talked. Neighbor met neighbor to thresh out dickers. Families who had grown up and separated to different parts of the country were brought in touch once more. And while the fiddles scraped and the guitar strings twanged and the partners swung around the floor, the news and the gossip of all four corners of the region shuttled back and forth.

When Lin and Gracie arrived, the dance had already been started and the first few numbers run off. The judge wandered over to meet some old friend and promptly began to talk water. Lestrade, bowing and shaking hands, was occupied for a moment. But he shook himself free from the crowd to overtake Gracie and lay a hand on her shoulder.

"Gracie, I'm going to demand the privilege of this first dance. Lin, he's a patient fellow and can wait."

"Mr. Lestrade, I'm sorry. I gave him the first two. We always dance the first two. If you'd care to have the third—"

For once in his life Lestrade made a poor show. He bobbed his head up and down and said, "Certainly," in a half-angry tone and wheeled away. Lin, suppressing a smile, led Gracie into the moving couples.

"He's got no right using my first name like that!" said she, flaring up. "I don't like it."

Lin didn't answer, being too busy taking care of himself and his partner. There were a great many other things in the world he did better than dancing. Unlike most men of the valley, he had been left alone at an early age and in the years that followed he had fended for himself at almost every outdoor job. In fact, only since Gracie Henry's smile had securely captured him had he been inside a dance hall. Therefore, he often missed the beat of the music and he would shuffle one foot, then the other, while the sweat worked up above his collar and he swore savagely to himself. But Gracie never seemed to mind. She hummed the tune with the fiddles and she cast her shining eyes on this couple and that, always thoroughly enjoying herself.

Yet, this evening, as their first dance ended and the second one began, she seemed to lose a measure of her happiness. Her eyes clouded and presently she raised her hand to Lin's arm, speaking in a puzzled manner.

"Lin, why are folks looking at us so queerly? I've caught several doing it. Seems like they won't meet my eyes, either. Is there something wrong with my dress?"

Lin Ballou evaded her glance. "Why, no, Gracie. You

look as pretty as a picture, and that's a fact. Guess they wonder why you put up with my clodhopping."

"Don't be foolish. They've seen us before. No, it's not that. It gives me the strangest feeling."

Lin shut his mouth. He had noticed this attention the moment he entered the schoolhouse, and quickly divined what it meant. The news of Offut's rebuff had got this far and passed from ear to ear. The thought of it filled him with anger that he struggled to suppress. He lost the sound of the music and brought up against a wall. Gracie stepped back, smiling at his awkwardness until she saw his face. Then the music stopped and Lestrade came up, once more his jovial self.

"No excuse this time, Gracie. It's the third dance." He led her away into the trouping couples.

Lin, thankful for the respite, moved toward the door and bumped against a freckled, red-thatched fellow of his own age.

"Hello, Pete," he said.

"'Lo," Pete said coolly, and moved off.

Lin made his way into the open and through a lane of trees to the gathered wagons. Wiping his forehead, he sat down on a tongue and stared across the valley to where the dim outline of the mesa stood forth. There was no moon and the scattered stars gave no light to the earth. Yet he could see in his mind every outline of that mesa, every trail and gully.

Maybe, he told himself, with a fresh touch of bitterness, I'd better saddle up and get back where I belong. Blamed little good I'll ever do by staying here now. Well, I got to play the hand out. Gracie, kid, your'e going to have a hard time . . .

A foot struck the wagon tongue and a match burst like a bomb directly in front. By the glow of it he saw Beauty Chatto's evil, swarthy face.

"Thinking it over, Lin?" the man asked in a voice thickened and blurred by whisky. "Coming 'round to my point of view? Better do it."

"Beauty, I'm not in any humor to be kidded. We threshed this matter out a couple hours ago."

Chatto had worked himself into a more belligerent frame of mind. "Now, look here, Lin, do you figure to declare war? Like I say, it don't do nothing but stir up trouble when a guy's got to fall back on gunplay, and I'd just as soon live and let live. But me and Nig is tired of your snooping. Gimme an answer now. Peace or trouble?"

"Going into the mesa tomorrow, Beauty. That's my answer."

"All right, by God!" Chatto growled. "You made yourself a bed to lie in. I'm serving notice now. Nig and me will shoot on sight."

Lin was silent for a time. "All right, Beauty," he said finally. "Have it your own way. But you better be well covered when you start the fireworks."

Suddenly his attention was diverted to the schoolhouse. The music had stopped some time back and a man's voice had taken up the interval. Lin, preoccupied with other matters, had given it little consideration. Now, as the voice stopped, it seemed as if bedlam had broken loose. A tremendous cheering burst out, from both men and women. Somebody rushed from the place and fired a gun. Feet stamped on the floor and the board walls rattled under pounding fists. Lin and Chatto, moved by a common curiosity, walked back to the door and looked in.

The crowd was packed loosely toward one end of the hall where James J. Lestrade and the judge were standing on chairs. The judge's face was scarlet with satisfaction, and Lestrade had his fingers hooked in his vest, beaming at everybody. After a while the noise quieted down and he spoke what appeared to be the last words of a speech.

"And so, as our good friend Judge Henry has said, we're on the road to prosperity at last. Let's set a formal meeting for tomorrow night at this same place and get every last homesteader to come. We'll draw up articles on the spot and then we'll start work. Why, folks, there's a fortune ahead for us all!"

Lin jumped through the door and up on a bench, shouting at the top of his voice to attract the crowd his way. "Wait a minute—wait a minute! Now, just before you folks all stampede toward this siren's call, I want to ask one question. Just one single question."

There was a quick switching of interest, a craning of heads. Even then he saw that nothing he might say would ever change their temper or subdue the leaping optimism in their hearts. They had fought so long with so little success; they had nourished the idea so tenaciously that some day water would come to them that now they were in but one state of mind. Judge Henry was swinging his hands up and down, on the verge of apoplexy. Lestrade had turned to frowning disfavor. In the moment's lull Lin put his question.

"I want to ask you folks this: Where—is the—money —coming from—for this project?" He spaced the words and emphasized them with a thrust of his finger. A murmur, a kind of breathless rustle went from man to man, and he hurried on. "How much do you think it costs to build an irrigation system? If the United States Government has passed us by, what makes you figure a parcel of green homesteaders can turn the trick?"

And then he was overwhelmed by such a shouting and booing as he had never before heard. It poured upon his head in ever-increasing force. As it died down, men began to move swiftly upon his vantage point, and he heard one voice and another saying, "What's biting your nose?" "You're no farmer—you're a prospector!" And at last came the words he had feared would come. "Go on back to your cows! Cows! Yeah—what brand do you like best?"

He saw Gracie Henry's face in that unreasoning multitude. Never before had it been so white and drawn. And right beneath his feet Beauty Chatto stared at him with mouth agape, like a man who has found his well formed opinions suddenly betray him. The foremost rank of men bore down, and Lin felt the bench sway. He was picked up bodily, struck at and badly shaken. Whirled around and shoved and pulled, he went staggering through the door, and then, as darkness protected him, he heard Lestrade's voice calling out. The men went inside and left him alone.

He spent a moment pulling his clothes back into shape. Then, sadly and quietly, he got his horse and turned homeward. Gracie would wonder what had happened—but the judge must take care of that. As for himself, there was but one thing left to do.

Well, they know how I feel about it, anyway, he thought. And some day those words will bear fruit. God, I'd like to find the man who shouted 'cows' at me! But the eggs are busted now, and maybe some good will come of it.

He reached his house, fried himself a meal and packed his lead horse. Within an hour he was striking eastward toward the high mesa, taking care now and then to stop and put his ear to the ground. He wanted no one following. What he was about to do had to be done without observation.

CHAPTER 4

NIGHT RIDERS

He traveled all that night, pushing the horses along at a steady pace. Beyond daylight he stopped for an hour's rest, ate a can of tomatoes, and continued easterly. The base of the mesa drew nearer and the ground grew more and more barren, seamed with dry creek beds and littered with boulders. It was a country beyond the power of any homesteader to improve, fit only for the poisonous creatures that crawled and burrowed in its sandy soil, and almost too dismal and desolate for the occasional passer-by.

But it's good for something, Lin reminded himself. The day's not far off when certain folks'll be tramping across it, bent on business.

Dusk found him camped on the first steep pitches of the mesa. And, as he had done a hundred times before in the same spot, he ate a cold meal in the dark and rolled up in his blankets twenty yards from the duffel, with the rifle close by.

Nor did he light a blaze in the morning, but journeyed on up the slopes until at last he stood on the mesa's rim and looked across a valley curtained by heat fog to that far-off irregular patch of earth representing Powder. The town did not hold his interest so much as a small trail of dust in the more immediate foreground, which, after a half hour's patient watching, proved to be the wake of a wagon going north on the Snake River Road. Thus satisfied, Lin left the panorama behind him, dipping into the corrugated sand and clay surface of the mesa.

Beauty Chatto'll probably be ahead of me, he mused. He's got a fresh horse and he always travels fast. Besides, he knew I was coming in right away, and it's natural he'd want to push in first. I'd better watch the front more.

He pulled the rifle from its boot and laid it across the saddle, studying the hilly contours that rose before him. It was a region admirably fashioned for ambuscade: at no place was there more than three or four hundred yards' level interval between the sudden convolutions of land. Ballou, on reaching some such eminence, had only a partial view of the way ahead before plunging down into the succeeding hollow. Thus he proceeded.

Toward noon he changed his direction and began a zigzagging from right to left. One particularly bald and prominent dome was the mark by which he steered, although instead of going straight toward it he bore well off to the right and dismounted. Nearby, on a small knoll, he lay for twenty minutes or so, sharply scanning the adjoining ridges. Satisfied that he wasn't being watched, he made a complete circle of the dome and then struck directly down a gully. Presently horses and rider dropped out of sight; the gully shot downward at a sharp angle and a draught of air struck Ballou's face. Turning a shelf of rock, he found himself before a cave that was high enough and wide enough to admit both himself and his two animals. Riding into it, he came to a stop and got down.

A more secluded spot could not have been found in

all the mesa. The location and shape of it concealed him from any eye, nor could it be discovered by chance way-farers, unless through blind accident they might have followed the tortuous path around the dome and down the gully.

The ashes of many campfires littered the floor. A little farther back a table and chairs of lodgepole had been constructed, and still rearward were two bunks, built against the rock wall. It was quite evidently a ren-dezvous of some permanence, and to Lin at least it was a home hardly less important in the last several weeks than his own down in the sultry valley. Stripping the horses, he picketed them at the mouth of the cave, fed them and then built a small fire over which he cooked himself the first good meal in two days. The supply of provisions he stowed away in a kind of rock cupboard. After smoking a reflective cigarette, he turned in for a sound sleep, the rifle within arm's reach.

He awoke, fresh and bouyant, well before dawn. Going to the cave's entrance, he saw the stars gleaming, bright and cold, and heard the swishing of the wind as it passed directly over the gully. The horses moved pa-tiently around their pickets. The nearer rubbed his muz-zle against Lin's shirt and pulled at the rope.

"Boy," Lin said, running a hand along the animal's neck, "you get a rest today, which I reckon you won't mind at all. When it comes to slogging along without complaint you'd make most any critter on two legs ashamed of himself. Get out of my pocket, you rascal, I haven't got an ounce of sugar. If I hadn't been rushed away from the valley so sudden like, I might've thought to bring some. But that's not our fault either. Anyhow, oats'll have to hold you for a spell. Now, let's get to business."

The affair at the schoolhouse still rankled when he

thought of it. But here in the cold, crisp dark, surrounded on all sides by the mystery of nature's handiwork, and catching at intervals the strong, aromatic scent of pine and sage, he was soothed to a certain degree of tranquillity. The mesa never failed him when he had asked peace and comfort of it. Towering high above the valley's heat and the valley's strife, it was a sure and swift healer of souls. To Lin Ballou it was a refuge where he might be thrown back to his own resources and for a time live in the closest contact with the earth.

But this day he had business to do. To the east, morning thrust its first dim beam of light above the horizon. Turning back, Lin kindled a fire and made himself flapjacks and coffee. He gave both horses a good measure of oats and saddled the riding animal. From the rock cupboard he drew a bottle and a few small pieces of iron. Thrusting them in his pocket, he stamped out the fire and led the way up the gully. There was need this day for a good deal of speed. Mounting, he swung east once more and began a long journey around the bald dome. It was somewhat cold. Throwing away his cigarette, he drew up the collar of his coat and broke into a subdued lament about the cowboy who wished to be buried in the lone prairie. The pony stuck up his ears and moved with sure feet among the rocks.

To Lin Ballou it was familiar country. The map of it stood quite plainly in his mind. On his right hand, not more than a mile distant, he might find a bunch of Double Jay stock. To the left, double that distance, was the summer ground of W. W. Offut's brand—that very same gentleman who had refused to speak to him in Powder. And at various parts of the mesa other herds were grazing. Farther east the mesa took a sharp drop and merged with the Flats.

At this particular time he had another point of the

41

mesa in mind. In the paling shadows a clump of trees stood silhouetted by themselves, and toward this he moved. Within twenty feet of them he left the horse and crawled upward until he had gained a place somewhat sheltered by their spindling trunks. Directly before him the land formed another of the innumerable hollows to be found throughout the mesa's extent. More interesting to Lin was the glow of a campfire in the pit of that hollow. He settled down to a steady observation.

Well, Nig Chatto's there, anyhow, he decided. Probably Beauty, too. Stands to reason he hoofed it back as fast as he could. Damn fools, they haven't got a mite of caution any more. Why don't they change their camp once in a while?

The answer, he told himself, was that they had scarcely anything to fear. It was a remote spot, not visited by line riders. Moreover, the Chattos had a kind of cunning about their methods that made them extremely bold. Nothing of an incriminating nature would ever be found around their fire. The work they did was accomplished elsewhere.

The sky turned from deep blue to gray and in quick succession to azure and rose. Fixed within the shelter of the trees, Lin watched the camp below. Presently he saw Beauty Chatto roll out of his blankets and sit before the fire. Nig, a figure somewhat smaller and less ugly than his brother, was already by the blaze, making breakfast. Their horses were picketed near at hand.

Satisfied with his discovery, Lin crawled back down the slope and swung into the saddle. This time he retraced a part of his trail to the cave and then forked off into another gully and rose rapidly, with no great caution, upward and to the north. In half an hour this took him to the commanding point of the entire mesa from which he might observe and—if anyone might be straying in the neighborhood—be observed. Shading his eyes, he spent a few moments surveying the distant hollows. At one particular point he found what he wished to see. Over there, browsing quietly, was one herd of W. W. Offut's stock. "Get along, Brimstone," he told the horse. And he thought: Let's see, this is Tuesday. Offut's riders don't come around this way until tomorrow. That leaves us clear. Quick and quiet does it if it's to be done at all. I can take care of the Chattos, but I don't want to fight any of Offut's buckaroos. "Step, Brimstone."

He put in a half hour traversing the rolling ground. Passing over a hillock, he drove his horse directly into a herd of browsing cattle.

As quick as he wished to be, he spent considerable time cutting out the particular animals he wanted. His rope sailed through the air and brought one such to a standstill. Down she went with Ballou out of the saddle and running over to tie her feet. Collecting a few pieces of grass and limbs, he lit a fire, heated an iron and then began a careful job of changing the existing brand to one of his own. Being a careful workman, he finished the work of the iron with a few drops of acid from the bottle in his pocket and stepped back to survey the result.

If anybody can spot a change he's got eyes like an eagle, he told himself. That ought to fool the sharpest stockyard inspectors.

He treated three more in the same manner and then returned the acid and iron to his pocket. Drawing the beeves clear of the herd, he pushed them up and over the ridge and headed them north as fast as they would go.

These daylight jobs are sure ticklish, he thought, looking anxiously behind. Now, if some crazy fool puncher should be ambling around at the wrong time . . .

The cows trotted up a slope and veered off, breaking into a gallop. Ballou reached for his gun, but too late. Beauty Chatto stood up from a boulder and grinned from ear to ear, both revolvers drawn.

"Climb down, Lin, climb down. I want to parley."

Ballou sat still, face impassive. "What's wrong, Beauty? One gun not enough to flag me?"

Chatto guffawed. "Not for you, Lin, not for you. When a man's caught with another gent's beef he's apt to be plumb desperate. Climb down, Lin. Why, you reckless sonofabitch, don't you know no better'n to frame yourself up on the summit in broad day? Where you figure folks keep their eyes?"

Lin shook his head, dismounting. "Folks ain't supposed to be around here today."

"Yeah? So you've got the buckaroos all doped out, too? Well, you forgot old Beauty. I'm always looking around. I see more'n that eagle up there does. But, say, I reckon I owe you an apology. Had you figured for a spy sure enough. Couldn't have told me different for a million pesos. Then I see the ruckus you caused over at the dance and hear all them harsh words tossed at you, and that sets me to wondering. Well, when old Beauty starts to wondering, something's bound to happen. So I set out to catch you and you make it all the easier by exposing yourself like a greenhorn fool. Lin, I thought you was honest, damned if I didn't. The apologies is all mine."

"Put down your guns, Beauty," Lin said. "I'll behave. What's the answer now? You turned honest yourself?"

"Me? Haw-haw-haw! I wish Nig could hear that!" Chatto studied Lin with his bold eyes. "I'll drop 'em, Lin, if you won't get sassy. Gimme your word, now."

"You've got it. Meanwhile those cows are heading back to the herd. What's your game?"

Chatto returned the guns and squatted on the ground. He drew a figure in the dirt with his stubby finger and seemed to be thinking of something. "Kid, there ain't room for *three* rustlers on this mesa. That's going to ruin a good thing. I dunno where you hide your stuff or how you get rid of it—but I can think of a better way right off."

"Yeah?"

"Why not hook up with Nig and me?"

"What for?" Lin demanded skeptically.

"Protection. Big money. You ain't running more'n three-four critters a week from the looks of things. Mebbe less. Nig and I are in for a big cleaning. Then you can't get much satisfaction doing everything by yourself. Three of us now, would be a fine outfit."

"Split three ways?" Lin said. "Share alike?"

Chatto drew another set of figures in the dirt before he answered. "No, Lin, it don't work thataway. It'd work out something like this: Profits is divided half and half. Out of one of those halves you and me and Nig split even, three ways."

"So?" Lin said. "Now I'm not a bit curious, Beauty. I didn't start this party. But such being the figures, I can't help seeing that there's another skunk or two in the woodpile. Who's so important as to draw down half of our plunder?"

Chatto turned reticent. "Somebody's got to market the stuff, Lin. And that's mighty dangerous for the gent in question."

Lin shook his head, dubious. "I like all the cards on the table. What am I to know about this other fellow? It looks plumb funny."

Chatto, in turn, was reluctant. "It ain't my part to spill his name, Lin. I got to see him first. Never mind. Don't let that worry you. Point is, we need another partner to do the riding and watching. You're a clever fellow, no mistake, and Nig and me'd be plumb agreeable. Far as money goes, you'll do better with us than without us. Anyhow, it's a cinch we can't be working separate."

Lin Ballou was silent for some length of time. "I'm in," he agreed finally. "But I've got to finish this particular job. Meanwhile, you see this other party. I don't like to work with a fellow until I know his brand of liquor."

Beauty Chatto rose, grinning. "We'll sure make a cleaning. Now let's split. There's a bunch of this gent's stock going into Portland a week from now. That's the time we get busy and do our chores, changing the brand and slipping them in with his critters. Meet Nig and me over there where them six pines stand up."

"All right," Lin agreed. He swung into the saddle and started back for the cattle. "A week from tonight. So long."

Night found him traveling again, this time with both horses, striking straight across the mesa and down the eastern slope into the Flats. After leaving Chatto, he had picked up the four cows and hazed them five miles or better from their original grounds and left them in a particularly remote and rugged section of the country. Chatto had returned toward the six pines, but Lin, ever watchful, had made a particular point of surveying all points of the compass before revisiting his cave.

Equally cautious was his night trip into the Flats. Instead of going in a direct line, which would have brought him close to the Chatto camp, he wasted the better part of two hours in detouring southward. By the time the stars all came out he was a great distance down the bench and many miles removed from the scene of the day's work.

As he traveled he caught sight of a locomotive headlight far across the Flats, hardly more than a pin-prick in the gloom. Presently that winked out and left him with no evidence of human company in all the vast extent of the land ahead. The wind sprang up and the coyotes commenced their dismal yammering on all sides of him. Now and then he flushed a jackrabbit from its shelter, at which the faithful Brimstone snorted a little and danced aside. Otherwise he rode in lonely silence, broken only by his own casual remarks to the horse.

When at last he reached the low ground it was nearing midnight and here he displayed once more the extraordinary caution that had been with him ever since leaving the valley. Dismounting, he slipped away into the darkness, crouched against the ground and surveyed the dim distances for fifteen or twenty minutes. The result was satisfactory. Returning to the pony, he changed his course somewhat and went at a faster pace. Thus, in two hours he sighted the vague outlines of a water tank standing alone on the desert. From the tank came the steady dripping of water. He stopped and whistled softly.

Out of the shadows he had his answer. "Yeah, Lin?"

"Uh-huh. Glad you got back on time. Thought maybe you'd have difficulty getting off the train. Saw its headlight from the bench and it didn't seem to stop."

A man's boot clanked on the iron rails and presently Lin had the silhouette of an extremely tall, thin body by his side. He got down and gripped the newcomer's hand. A slow, drawling voice pronounced a few non committal words.

"Had a difficult time and that's a fact. Come on the freight so I wouldn't attract attention. Gave the brakie five dollars to drop me off here, but the engineer was trying to make time across this level piece so I had to jump for it. Scattered my luggage a hundred yards. Busted all my cigars and left me in a right mean temper towards all railroads. Fact. Hope the engine busts a gadget and the crew has to walk home."

Lin chuckled. "Keep your temper, Bill." He drew up the lead horse and spoke with sudden eagerness. "Don't hold back the important news. What's the verdict?"

A long arm draped itself across Lin's shoulder. "Fellow, it's the true dope. So far as we've gone, everything is pay dirt, a mile wide and a mile deep. Prospects? By god, the prospects are amazing. If the next few places we tackle show the same result, there'll be plenty of backing just as soon as we need it. How's that?"

Lin took off his hat and sighed profoundly. "I could kiss a sheep, Bill. Happy days! But we're going to have to move fast. There's a fly in the gravy."

The tall man grunted. "What's the matter?"

Lin squatted on his heels and related the irrigation boom in a few terse, disgusted words. "Now you see what's going to happen? This water company will get everything all cluttered up with its ditches and laterals. First thing you know there'll be a lot of money sunk uselessly. When the time comes for us to start our little venture, it's going to be that much more expensive on all hands and the cook. I tried to head them off but the crooked rascal who's heading the thing yelled me down."

"Who?"

"James J. Lestrade, no less."

Bill whistled. "Lin, I heard something at the main office concerning that gent. Maybe he ain't just interested in water, either."

Lin stood up. "Think he's got wind of this same idea of ours?"

"I'd bet a hundred dollars he has."

Lin was silent for a time, trying to reconcile this news with Lestrade's interest in water. "Can't just see how he figures to join the two," he said at last.

"Devious ways have a manner of joining, some time or later," the lanky Bill observed. "Let's get somewhere. I'm dying to smoke."

"Jump on the horse. You'll have to ride him bareback."

Bill collected his luggage and put a leg up. "What's our next move?"

Lin Ballou led the way north, parallel with the mesa. "We'll reach that old Miller house—it was abandoned last fall, you remember—by daylight. Then we'll stay over till it's dark again. All the ground we've got to cover now is close to Powder and it means night work and plenty of caution. Ought to get it finished in four-five days, shouldn't we?"

"Uh-huh."

"Then," Lin went on, sweeping the darkness with watchful eyes, "you can hoof it back to headquarters and get the final decision. We've got to move pretty fast from now on. While you're gone, I've got other irons to heat."

"Lead on," Bill urged. "I want to get to shelter where I can light a smoke. I'm dying for a little nicotine in my system."

Within forty-eight hours of this meeting at the water tank, Beauty Chatto himself had reason to engage in a similar rendezvous after dark, conducted with the same careful maneuvering. Sliding down the westward slope of the mesa in the late afternoon, he rode with the reckless speed so characteristic of him for several hours, gradually aiming toward Lestrade's Double Jay home ranch in the southward. About two miles short of this point, and late at night, he arrived at a deserted nester's shanty and halted. Within the walls of this rickety affair he smoked several cigarettes and through the window watched the outline of the nearest hummock of land. After about an hour of this vigil he was rewarded by the swift patter of a rapidly traveling horse. A shadow passed across the horizon and dipped down, out of sight.

A heavy voice said, "Ho, you fool horse," and wheeled directly by the shanty door, at the same time calling out in no particularly subdued tone, "You there, Chatto?"

Beauty moved from the shanty, grumbling. "Damn it, Lestrade, ain't you never going to take care how you talk? Folks can hear you a mile away."

Lestrade sat in the saddle. "Been a policy of mine to let folks know I'm present, so it's kind of difficult to tone down. Don't you worry, Chatto. Nobody around this neck of the woods."

"Can't tell about that," Chatto said. "Folks is often where they ain't got no business being. For instance, you and me."

"Well, now, I wouldn't say we've got no business here. Fact is, we have some right important business."

"All set for next Tuesday, like you said?"

"That's right. How you coming?"

"Fair enough. We'll have nigh forty head."

Lestrade said, "Uh-huh," in a pleased tone and, much to Chatto's disgust, lit a cigarette. "You drive 'em down to the East Flats loading pens Tuesday night. My cows'll be already there. I'll jerk everybody away from the place except the foreman and a right close-mouthed man. Wednesday they'll be shipped. Think you can do it in time?"

"Sure. We got an addition to our happy family."

Lestrade jerked the cigarette from his mouth and said, "Who's that?" in a savage voice. "Addition? You fool, you mean to say you took in another partner? Without my knowledge?"

"Oh, I ain't told him nothing about your connection with us. He knows there's another party—name unknown. I said I'd see said party before giving out any

50

more information. But, you see, this fellow's in our own line of business and we can't have no opposition. That'd create a fuss sooner or later. Easiest thing was to take him in. Besides, Nig and me, we needed a little more help."

"Who is he?"

"Brace yourself for a shock," Chatto warned, grinning through the dark. "The gent is none other than your friend Lin Ballou."

"By Godfrey!" Lestrade exclaimed in complete amazement. "Lin—why, Lin—I thought he was honest. You must be joking."

"The joke's on us. I figured him honest, too. But after that affair at the dance, and after I caught him red-handed, tampering with some of Offut's critters, I sure changed my mind."

Lestrade was lost in several moments' silence. The horse moved beneath him uneasily. "No, I didn't figure him to be a rustler. But I did figure he had something else on his mind besides prospecting. That's just a blind."

Chatto muttered something to himself, and then broke out with a dissatisfied remark. "Well, there may be something else he's got in his system, for all I know. Blamed if I can just figure what. But I never take a man's word for granted till I do a little investigating on my own hook. So after catching him with Offut's critters, I figured I'd follow him and see what he did next. What do you suppose it was?"

Lestrade, moving nervously, urged Chatto on. The cigarette made a crimson arc through the air and fell amid a tiny shower of sparks.

"Well, sir, I followed him back a piece on the mesa and then I lost him. Yes, by God, he plumb vanished in the earth. Well, I wait. Bye and bye he comes out of the same hole he goes into—this is after dark—and I track him down into the East Flats and lose him again. But next morning I find his tracks extending over to the water tank and back towards Miller's old place. I didn't go no farther. But there's sign that says he met another gent by that tank. I see the footprints. Now what's that mean?"

Lestrade had grown more and more restive as Chatto related his story. After Beauty stopped he leaned over in the saddle and put a heavy hand on his shoulder and spoke in a half-angry manner.

"Beauty, he's got to be stopped. You understand? He's got to be put away. There's too much at stake for him to be meddling."

"Meddling how?" Chatto demanded.

"Never mind," Lestrade replied. "He's up to another game and I know what it is. If he's let alone he'll ruin old James J. Lestrade. He's got to be stopped."

"Well, old-timer, if you want a bust of gunplay from Beauty, you'll have to pay high."

"Come here close," Lestrade said. Chatto bent forward. Lestrade, dropping his head still lower, began to whisper.

Chatto said "Uh-huh" at the end of each phrase and finally stepped back. "You want him double-crossed, huh?"

"Well, that'll clear anybody else of suspicion. Old man Offut's on the warpath, looking for rustlers, and if he catches Lin that'll leave you all the better off, won't it?"

"You got a head," Chatto said in admiration. "In plain words, you want Lin Ballou's neck stretched? You want him killed?"

Lestrade swore. "Be careful of your words!"

"Oh," Chatto said, "you might as well say it outright if you mean it. If it's crooked work, it's crooked work."

Lestrade rested a moment, quite still. Then he nodded slowly. "That's it."

"All right. Leave it to me. You take care of your end of it."

Lestrade turned about and galloped away. Chatto watched him climb to the rim of the hummock and drop from sight. Slowly he went to his own horse and started back for the mesa.

Life is sure getting complicated for a plain rustler like me, he brooded. There's something else going on that I don't savvy. Them gents is playing at another game. Beauty Chatto, you sure better watch your hole card or you'll get tangled up in trouble. But if Lestrade wants Ballou outa the way, outa the way he goes. G'long pony.

CHAPTER 5

THE STORM GATHERS

Coming out of the mesa the following Sunday, Lin Ballou arrived in front of Hank Colqueen's ranch to find that slow-moving, sunburned giant still tugging away at his fence wire, some distance farther down the Snake River Road. Halting to exchange gossip, Lin was shrewd enough to perceive that the man was far less amiable than on preceding occasions, a fact he stored away in his memory as just another omen of his own increasing unpopularity. This, however, he found not to be the whole reason, for he had not passed a dozen words when Hank turned to the ever-present subject of water and the irrigation project.

"Working on it already?" Lin asked, a little surprised. "Why, it hasn't been more than a week since you fellows got the idea in your heads."

"Sooner we start, the sooner we'll get water," Colqueen replied, abandoning his wire-puller. "Got the makings? I ain't been to Powder for supplies nigh onto a month." He took sack and papers from Lin, his fiery red face all furrowed in scowls.

"I saw a whole line of wagons striking across the desert," Lin said. "Looks like they're taking a powerful lot of supplies into Lake Esprit."

Colqueen stopped midway in the process of building his cigarette and turned a fretful countenance on Lin. "Yeah, they are taking a lot of supplies in. You know why?"

"Uh-uh."

"Well, I'll tell you," Colqueen said, displaying rare belligerence for a man who usually was so serene and imperturbable. "The damn fools up there got careless and had a fire. Burned down their storehouse. Lost all the tools and grub. Three thousand dollars went up in smoke, night before last." He stared across the flat waste of land. "It makes me plumb sick to think of it. Three thousand dollars, Lin! Why, that's a small fortune to us fellows. And nary a cent's good come of it. Yes, sir, when I heard of it I pushed my dinner plate away and almost bawled. Money ain't that easy to get."

"You got stock in the proposition?" Lin asked.

"Sure have. I raised five hundred dollars."

"Hank, you must have been hoarding all that wealth."

"Slapped a mortgage on the place," Hank said gloomily. "Took me five years to clear it of debt and then I go and get myself right back in. Bank in Powder wouldn't take it, but there was an agent from a Portland corporation hereabouts that swung the deal for me and a bunch of other folks. Oh, I don't regret the money. It's for a good cause. But sometimes I have my doubts about the management."

"Why?" Lin said swiftly.

"Well, they might have hired valley folks to do the digging and general work. That would have kept the money circulating here. But no, they wouldn't do that. Had to go over to the Coast and import a lot of Chinamen. Work lots cheaper, they said."

"Whose idea was that?"

"Lestrade's, I reckon. We made him general manager, with Judge Henry as sort of a president of the board. The judge, he balked on that idea, too, but come around to Lestrade's way of thinking, finally. Oh, maybe the man's right. I try to keep an open mind on the subject. Cheapest way is the best way—but damn it, a fellow don't like to see foreigners lopping around the landscape, taking the bread and butter out of his mouth."

"Huh," Lin said reflectively.

He went on, forgetting to take the makings with him, forgetting to ask the news of the outside world. Here was fodder onough for his mind to keep him in a dark study all the way down the road to his own place. He was still turning it over, with increasing distrust for the whole affair, when, some time in the afternoon he drew up before the Henry ranch.

Gracie and the judge were sitting in the shade of the porch, and it made Lin forget the troublous news when he saw her. He carried the picture of this girl with him always. It made little difference whether he rode in the heat of the day or camped at night beside some solitary fire on the high mesa; this straight and sturdy figure with the clear, frank eyes and the welcoming smile was an almost constant companion in his mind. Not that Lin Ballou was an overly sentimental fellow; he distinctly was not. His early training had brought him so close to the hardships and cruelties of a new, raw land that he had been whipped into a hard, self-reliant, practical man. But even so, Gracie Henry meant a lot to him and his spirits always rose when he came to the Henry place. A broad, cheerful grin lighted his face as he swung down, dusted himself and walked over to the porch.

"Howdy, folks. Gracie, you look prettier than any picture. Always do. You're the one gal in this climate who seems to thrive on sand and heat."

Gracie tucked an arm around his elbow. "If you had to see me every day you'd not be so complimentary. Any girl's face looks good after a week of jackrabbits."

"Now that," Lin said, "is a shocking statement for you to make. Judge, you're the same amiable gentleman as always. Hope the new water system progresses in a satisfactory manner."

"Hem," the judge said irritably.

Lin's pleasantry had been purely for effect. It took but a single glance to see that the judge had aged perceptibly in the short term of a week. The skin of his puffy face looked more sallow than usual, and a heavy cloud of worry dulled his eyes. He was not the type to bear up well under great responsibility. The man's egotism fed on neighborly praise, and now that he was hearing from certain disgruntled settlers like Hank Colqueen, he grew morose and more sarcastic.

"Understand there's been a slight bonfire up the line," Lin continued by way of making talk. He settled himself on the porch steps in a manner that he might command Gracie's face as she rocked in the chair.

"What of it?" Judge Henry snapped. "Godamighty, don't fires come to all places? Unavoidable accident."

"Sure, sure," Lin soothed. "Some of the boys, I hear, don't like the Chinese coming in."

"Can't please everybody," was Henry's tart reply. "I thought the men of this valley were responsible people. Half of them are nothing but children. Always complaining. We are doing the best we can—myself and Mr. Lestrade. When this project's finished they'll have me to thank for most of it, but I doubt if they'll ever give me any thanks. That's gratitude for you! Another time and I shall know better than to try to help such fools."

"Father," Gracie said quietly, "that's an unkind word to use on your neighbors."

"Fools!" Judge Henry repeated with more emphasis.

"Who," Lin asked after some moments of thought, "takes care of the money?"

"It's in the Powder bank," the judge said. "Mr. Steele is paymaster. A suggestion *I* made."

The girl rose. "You're going to town, aren't you, Lin? Well, you wait a minute while I saddle Vixen and I'll go with you. I have some shopping to do."

The judge spoke out with unusual vigor and frankness. "Gracie, you want to remember I've got a reputation to maintain. There's entirely too much talk—"

Gracie hushed him with a single, swift, half-angry glance. So unusual was it for her to lose her temper that the judge subsided, grumbling. Lin checked a hot volley of words and walked to his horse. He had put up with a great deal of unfriendliness from the judge and a great deal of outright scorn. Of late, that unfriendliness had greatly increased, and Lin, in spite of his attempt at an easygoing manner with the man, had been sorely galled. Only Gracie's presence and Gracie's timely intervention kept him discreet.

Gracie rode up, and together they swung away from the house and down the highway.

"Your dad," Lin said, "has got too much on his chest. This water deal won't help him any."

"Don't I know it!" Gracie replied strongly. "He hasn't been himself a moment since it started. Lin, I'm worried. Every day it seems something's gone wrong or some one of the valley folks comes to quarrel. How I wish Mr. Lestrade had never employed the Chinese. You can't imagine how bitter it made everyone feel. It may save money, but it won't save tempers."

They turned around a clump of poplars and came upon a tall, sprawling piece of machinery planted not far from the road. It was an immense ditch digger with long arms and an endless chain of buckets. A plume of steam hissed out of a pipe and a group of men loitered on its shady side. Behind it trailed a wake of upturned earth.

"There," Gracie said, "is another piece of trouble. Mr. Lestrade had a construction company rush that down here immediately. It dug a few yards of ditch and broke. Now they've got to wait for spare parts from Portland, while the whole crew sits in the shade and draws pay."

"Meanwhile, also," Lin noted as they passed by, "it burns fuel in a completely unnecessary manner."

"They say they must keep the boiler in shape."

Lin nodded. "They would say that. Gracie, girl, there's more in this than meets the naked eye."

"What do you mean, Lin?"

He didn't answer, and for the rest of the trip into Powder they were altogether silent. Once in town they separated, agreeing to meet again at the end of twenty minutes. Lin tied his horse by the general store and crossed to the postoffice for his mail. This time, he noted, the hatchet-faced purveyor of letters literally threw the mail through the wicket and slammed it shut, all without comment. Being an equable-minded fellow, Lin mustered a slight grin and went out to the street. With the exception of one particular letter, he dismissed the collection as unimportant. This letter he held up to the light, and then tucked it into his pocket without opening it.

Company's directions to Bill, I guess, he surmised.

His next move was to loiter down the street to a point opposite James J. Lestrade's office and stare through the window in an absent-minded manner. The place was empty, but in the adjoining office he had a glimpse of Dan Rounds, half asleep with his feet cocked up on the table.

Somebody mentioned Dan as being lawyer for this irrigation project, he recalled. Well, there's one honest man connected with this deal, anyhow.

Mulling over this haphazard conjecture, he passed to the shady side of the street and walked by the bank. It so happened that the cashier, Archer Steele, was near the plate glass window, idly staring into the dusty thoroughfare. He looked sharply at Lin Ballou. His sharp, preternaturally sober face kept its expression, and the slaty, cautious eyes did not betray even a flicker of recognition. Lin passed on with a small excitement rising in his breast. The suspicion which had been slowly working in him all during the day rose to higher pitch, and he found himself saying over and over again, to himself, Treasurer, is he? That man's crooked—dead crooked! He's crooked, damn it!

Dropping into the store, he gave an order for supplies as usual. This time, after the sack had been filled and passed to him, Stagg, the proprietor, cleared his throat and spoke somewhat nervously.

"Mr. Ballou—Lin—you know times is pretty hard with

59

us folks. Let's see, your account's run two months now, ain't it? I was wondering if you could pay something down. Of course—"

Lin stared at Stagg in a manner that confused him and made him forget the gist of his request.

"If you mean pay up," Lin said, "why don't you come round to it in less words? Habit in these parts is to pay three-month stretches, ain't it? That's the way you and I have done business for eight years."

"Times," the storekeeper repeated doggedly, "are getting hard."

"Far as this valley is concerned," Lin remarked, reaching into his pocket, "they never were anything but hard. Don't worry, Stagg, you'll never lose a cent from me— or get another one." He threw two gold pieces on the counter, and the groceryman's hand fell eagerly over them.

The man pawed around a till for the proper change, meanwhile protesting, "Don't take it unkindly, Lin. But —you know—"

"I know there's a good deal of talk going around which concerns me," Lin said. "If that's biting you, all right. This valley is so soured on itself that a bee would die of poisoning if it stung anybody."

With that pronouncement he walked out in no favorable frame of mind. Nor was he to fare better outside, for on emerging from the store he came directly upon Gracie Henry and W. W. Offut. Gracie broke off in the middle of a sentence to speak to Lin.

"I'm through now if you are."

"All set," Lin said.

Offut straightened his great body and directed a steady gaze at Lin. The man had an extremely serious face and a pair of steel-blue eyes. When he turned them on any particular object they had all the effect of a brace

60

of guns. Extremely few people had withstood those eyes, and none wished to arouse the temper behind them. No other man in the breadth and length of the country was quite so much respected as W. W. Offut. He was rigidly honest, rigidly fair, and in the course of a long life he had personally tracked down a score of outlaws and cattle thieves. The rumor was that Offut, when a very young man, had killed an opponent with a single blow of his fist. No one knew the truth of the tradition, and no one ventured to ask. As for emotion, he rarely displayed it. He maintained a kind of stiff courtesy in all his dealings with others, except in one matter. Every time a baby was born in the county, W. W. Offut sent the parents twenty dollars' worth of groceries, and at some time, sooner or later, he was sure to come personally and tickle the infant with his own immense finger.

So much for the man who, by a single act, had sent rumors flying through the valley as to Lin Ballou's honesty. At the present moment his eyes rested unwaveringly on Lin, while the latter returned the glance with a clouded brow. Finally the cattleman nodded and doffed his hat to the girl, speaking courteously.

"Miss Gracie, you give your dad my particular respects and tell him I hope he will find his business goes along in good style." Inclining his head once more, he clapped on his hat and strolled away.

Gracie gathered her bundles and jumped into the saddle. Lin got to his own horse and they rode silently out of town. The girl maintained a puzzled, worried air and her cheeks glowed pink with some kind of emotion which she seemed to be fighting. At last, when they were a good mile down the highway she turned toward Lin and spoke frankly.

"If I hadn't seen with my own eyes I never, never would have believed it. All this foolish talk around the valley I would never listen to. But, Lin, you've got to be honest with me. Why should Mr. Offut treat you like that?"

"Not being on speaking terms with him, I couldn't tell you, Gracie."

"That's no answer. You must have an idea."

"Oh, I've got lots of ideas," Lin said, smiling a little.

"Well, then," she prompted.

Lin turned sober. "Gracie, I want you to trust me without asking too many questions. Maybe sometime I can answer them. But not now."

"It's not fair," she said bitterly. "How am I to answer all the sneers and whispers I hear about you? Why, my own father speaks of you as a common thief! How can I answer him when you tell me nothing? Must I stand by and let them run your reputation into the ground?"

Lin bowed his head. For a moment humor and courage deserted him, and he was on the point of defending himself. But with the words on his tongue he regained control. "Guess you'd better let them talk, Gracie. Talk's cheap."

"But your reputation isn't cheap," Gracie cried. "Tell me this—have you ever found the slightest trace of gold in the hills to justify your keeping on with the search?"

"There may be gold in the mesa," Lin said candidly, "but I've never spent a minute trying to find it."

"Then that's a cover-up for something else?"

"Yes, Gracie."

"And you can't tell me, can't trust me?"

"No, Gracie, I can trust you. I'd trust you to the end of the world—but it's not my part to tell you."

They rode in silence for a long, long time. "I won't ask you to tell me," she said at last. "But what about your land and your house? You haven't touched them for months. What will become of the place? What of your future, Lin?"

"Does that matter to you?"

The question brought a flush to her cheeks. Yet she was a girl of courage and she answered bravely enough. "You ought to know it does."

Lin slapped the saddle resoundingly. "Out of a very, very sad world that comes as the one mighty cheering piece of news. You take heart, Gracie. Things are coming to a head now, I think. It won't be long before I can tell you everything."

They were approaching the Henry place. Gracie was as solemn and disturbed as he had ever seen her.

"I try to keep heart, Lin, but it seems as if every blessed thing is going wrong. Folks abuse you to my face. Dad's not himself, and somehow I mistrust everything Mr. Lestrade does or says. He comes too much to the place and every time he has some excuse to put his fat hand on my shoulder." The temper of this red-haired girl blazed up momentarily. "Some day I'll get a knife and cut his arm off!" Immediately she saw the utter foolishness of what she had said and smiled through her worries. "Oh, Lin, I don't mean to burden you with my troubles."

"I wish you could burden me more with them," Lin said. "Some day, if things go a little better, I'll ask that right."

"Lin," she said, a sudden gay laugh rippling up, "this is no place to propose, so be careful. I might fall on your neck. When will I see you again?"

He studied the high mesa, standing so isolated and cool in the distance. "Lord," he sighed, "I don't know. This week is going to be a humdinger. If all goes well, I'll be back in five-six days. If not—"

The tip of her finger rested on his hand a moment,

cool and reassuring. "Good-bye, then. And good luck."

She rode into the yard with a last wave, and Lin went on, thoughtful, sober.

Back in Powder, W. W. Offut strolled into the general store for a handful of cigars. Suddenly he was arrested by the groceryman's outstretched palm, in which glittered two gold pieces.

"See those?" Stagg said. "I got those from Lin Ballou in payment of his bill."

"Yes, sir," Offut replied in a kind of cool courtesy. He helped himself to the cigars and threw the change on the counter.

The storekeeper was not discouraged. "Well, it's gold, ain't it? And where would Lin get ready money? He never hesitated a minute to pay when I asked him, and I saw his wallet half full of money. He's got a ready supply. Don't that look suspicious?"

"Suspicious? Where is the suspicion, sir?"

Stagg began to be discouraged by Offut's distant manner. He had expected the cattleman to show curiosity. "Well," he continued somewhat lamely, "it looks suspicious. What with all these rumors flying around and considering how little Ballou works for a living, it *does* seem strange."

"How strange, sir?"

This persistent questioning began to make the storekeeper fearful. It was not his policy to speak openly unless he knew his confidant to be sympathetic. Born and bred in this land, he understood only too well the dire penalty of attacking a man's reputation. So he mumbled, "Well, I thought mebbe you'd be interested."

"Let me see the money, sir," Offut said, and the groceryman handed it over. Offut's cold blue eyes studied the coins a moment and then he passed them back. He lit a cigar, turned, and at the same time issuing a warning. "Men often find themselves in dangerous water from a loose tongue," he said, and left the store.

Offut made his way slowly down the street to the county courthouse, a small wooden building that served, in the lower part, as a center for the public business, and in the upper part, as a jail. Entering this, he found three other men, all about his age and all of his unquestioned honesty. They, too, were cattlemen and had been in the country from the very first. These three, with Offut, constituted a self-elected cattlemen's committee, and they immediately went into a kind of formal meeting.

"Rumors fly around this town as thick as mosquitoes," Offut said. "Stagg just now showed me two gold pieces Lin Ballou had given him. He as much as said that Lin had got them through selling beef."

One of the others spoke up. "Ballou's pretty well tarred with that suspicion, ain't he?"

"Yes. General opinion in the valley." Offut put on a pair of spectacles and drew a slip of paper from his pocket. "According to my foreman, I've lost something like thirty head of stock from the mesa these last four weeks. You boys are as bad off, I guess."

Another nodded. "Mine's a little less. Well, do we ride tonight?"

Offut nodded. "Lestrade says he's got a line on a party."

"Where did he get the dope?"

Offut shook his head. "Says he's got his own sources of information. Says he'll guarantee results. We'll ride with him. I'll bring along three-four of my own boys in case of trouble."

"Lestrade didn't mention names, eh?"

"None," Offut said. "Nor does he know of our particular agent in the matter."

The four of them exchanged significant glances, as if sharing a common, unspoken thought. Offut returned the paper to his pocket.

"We'd better start from my place soon as dark sets in. No need to caution you boys about quietness. Better take a little grub, too, because we'll have to lay over a day."

They filed out one by one and rode off into the valley by various roads, all aiming toward a common objective. Not long afterward James J. Lestrade galloped hastily into the town, spent a brief moment at his office and galloped as hastily out again, taking the trail toward Offut's ranch. He had strapped two revolvers around him.

CHAPTER 6

DISASTER

Lin Ballou started toward the mesa somewhat earlier than usual, and he traveled faster. Morning brought him to the bench and by noon he was at the cave. Bill, the lanky man he had brought across from the East Flats water tank, was there before him, just returned from an expedition of his own, and extremely elated. Lin gave him the letter and waited somewhat impatiently to know its contents. Bill tore it open and skimmed the writing with a rising eyebrow.

"Big boss says to hustle back this very minute with whatever dope I've picked up. Seems like there's a need for a decision."

"What's pushing him, I wonder?" Lin asked, staking the horses.

"Maybe there's other parties smelling this very same wind," Bill suggested, draping his frame on a bunk. "Can't keep a secret forever. How's tricks down below?"

"Water everywhere, but not a drop trickling into the valley yet. Lots of delay, lots of expense, and it all looks crooked to me. Sometimes I think I can see what Lestrade's aiming at and then again it's as dark as this here bosky dell."

"Speaking of which," Bill grumbled, "I've about got rheumatism from sitting around in this draught. A colder place there never was. Well, seeing as the boss is excited, I'd better make tracks for the water tank and catch a freight tonight. Number Ten stops for water. I'll ride a flat car."

"You'll have to hoof it," Lin said. "I've got to do a little piece of business tonight."

"Guess that won't kill me. I ain't set against using my feet like you valley boys are. A geologist does a lot of traveling on shank's mare. Let's see, that freight goes east an hour after the westbound hits the tank. Which would make it near three in the morning. All right, I'll start when dark comes."

Ballou had rolled into a blanket and was already half asleep. "All right, youngster," he murmured. "Now I've got to take a cat-nap. Dog-tired. Call me 'round six and have the waffles ready." With that he was lost to the world.

When his partner punched him in the ribs the long shadows were falling in the cave. A small fire burned brightly, and coffee fumes filled the area. Lin got up, took care of the horses and ate his flapjacks.

"I hate to think of you walking all that distance," he said. Tell you what—you take the pack horse and ride him to Latourelle's. Just ask Latourelle to keep him till he's called for. It'll be a half mile out of your way but you'll make a lot better time. Meanwhile, when do you think you'll get back?"

"According to prospects, in five-six days. That digging I did while you were away finished the job. Next time, I'll probably meet you right in Powder, ready to talk turkey."

"Make it in Powder, then, a week from this night. I'll be waiting."

"Check."

By the time they had finished their meal, securely put away all the provisions and packed Bill's kit bag, it was dusk. Lin saddled his horse, feeling considerable sympathy for the patient animal.

"When all this tramping around is over," he promised, "you're going to get a good, long rest, old fellow."

Leading the way up the gully, he guided Bill across the mesa in a southerly direction, and gave him a landmark to steer by until the misleading high country was well behind. They shook hands and parted.

Lin swung back, northward, and traveled as rapidly as the rough ground would permit. Within twenty minutes he was at the six pines and riding down into the small bowl occupied by the Chattos. A small fire gleamed like a yellow gem in the very pit of the depression, but when he came to it he found the place deserted. Not even a stray can nor so much as an extra piece of firewood gave evidence of its recent tenants.

Still in the saddle, Lin whistled softly and after quite some wait he heard stones rattling down the slope. A heavy body passed through the outer darkness and stopped at a safe distance.

"Come on up, boys," Lin said. "You know who I am."

"We damn near traveled without you," grumbled a voice which Lin immediately recognized as that of Beauty Chatto. "What took you so allfired long?" He moved into the circle of light, a somber, black-visaged creature. At times there was a measure of humanity in the man, a certain self-knowledge of his utter unscrupulousness. And usually he had a certain amount of humor about him. Tonight all this was lacking. He stared grimly at Ballou, as if weighing and judging him in the suspicious, uneven balance of his mind. "If a man's going to travel with me, he's got to be on the dot. Won't have you round the country, leaving me and Nig waiting. Where you been?"

Lin said evenly, "None of your business, Beauty. This is your proposition, not mine. If you figured last week I was safe enough to ride with, you better keep the same notion in your head tonight. Don't razz me. I don't take it well. You said to meet you after dark. This is the time and this is the place. But why advertise our location with the bonfire?"

"So you'd know we was waiting," Beauty said. He tramped the fire beneath his boots, leaving only a smoking mass that now and then emitted a fitful spark. "Come on. We've got a whole slough of work cut out for us, It's a long way to—" He checked himself as he led the way up the farther slope, found his horse and got into the saddle.

"To where, Beauty?"

"That's something you'll discover later."

"Still holding out on me, eh? Beauty, you'll have to come across with the whole works if I ride with you boys."

"You'll know it all by the time we're through with the present deal," Beauty said, not quite so gruff. "No time to parley now. Nig's up ahead waiting for us. Put the spurs into that donkey of yours."

The ugly man was in a hurry and, unusually for him, he seemed apprehensive. From time to time, as they forged over the rugged ground, Lin saw Beauty turn in the saddle and look behind him.

"Ain't nobody within ten miles," he said in a subdued rumble, "but I always like to watch the ridges, nevertheless. Don't do no harm. For God's sake, push that horse!"

"What's the program?" Lin asked.

"Nig's been doing a little cutting out. Started before dark. We won't have to do no milling around. Pick 'em up and haze 'em along fast as we can go. Run the fat right off the critters."

"Uh-huh," Lin said. His senses, sharpened by the nature of the work he was engaged in, suddenly took warning, and he drew up the horse. Beauty went on a few feet before stopping. Ahead at no great distance was the uneasy, shuffling sound of cattle. Out of the darkness floated a challenge.

"Beauty?"

"Yeah. Me and Lin. Set?"

"All tied up in a knot. Read to step on her?"

"Yeah," Beauty said. His arm scraped against the saddle. There was a sudden burst of match light. A blazing arc went upward to his face and touched a cigarette, then fell to the ground in a streak of vivid flame. Lin, roused, spurred his horse beside the outlaw and struck the cigarette from the man's mouth.

"Of all the bonehead tricks! Haven't you got a lick of sense? I thought you were an old hand at this. My

70

great aunt! I'm not traveling with any brass bands to-night. Cut it out!"

"Doggone it," said Beauty in a crestfallen tone, "that's sure one on me. Bonehead is right. Just wasn't thinking, Lin. Been so long since I had a smoke that it sorta come to me naturally, without thinking. Never mind. Ain't nobody near."

"That's what the bobcat thought when he stepped into the trap," Lin said, still angry.

"Let's go," Nig said. Being several feet away, Lin could see nothing of Beauty's brother, but he could hear the man's heavy breathing and the creak of his saddle leather. "Beauty and me had better ride flank. You haze 'em along from behind. Let's get outa here. If anything should go wrong, I'll let a yelp out of me, which is a sign for you to make a run for it."

The brothers moved away and presently were lost to Ballou. He rode down the slanting ground and came up behind the slowly moving cattle. From somewhere in the van he heard Beauty's softly spoken signal. "Let's go." At that he shoved his horse against the bunch and as gently as possible, pressed them on. They got in motion after some confused moving about. Lin was kept extremely busy for a few moments heading off bolters, but finally they settled to a steady pace. The run was on.

After they had gone some hundred yards Lin knew where he was. At this point the mesa curved into a kind of chute that led, with some amount of winding and twisting, out of the high ground and down into the East Flats. It was an admirable natural road to take stock over in the dark, for the banks of it acted as a check against the cattle breaking off on the flanks. In addition, this particular gully was the least obstructed of all the entrances or exits of the mesa. Therefore, it was possible to put the herd to a stiff run. They had not gone far before the whole group was a-trot. Lin sat losely in the saddle with little work to do and free to puzzle over the point they were bound for.

Beauty Chatto had said they shipped the rustled stock through another man—obviously some cattleman of the valley. That meant, of course, that eventually they would reach one of the three or four loading pens along the railroad. Lin had lived long enough in the country to know just how this worked, but it did not seem possible they would try to drive that whole distance in a night's time. For they still had the job of changing brands before them, and this had to be done in daylight, in some isolated section where chance travelers would be least apt to stray.

And what brand would they use? What cattleman acted as agent for the Chattos? Lin, running through the list in his mind, could not fix upon any particular man who would put himself in any such position. Obviously it was some extremely bold and restless character who paraded the streets of Powder and acted the part of honesty. Well, within a few hours he should know that man's name. And in all probability it would be one well known to him.

Folks rise and fall in this world, he mused, and that gent, whoever he may be, is leading straight for destruction. This tampering with right and wrong is a risky thing, always.

He sat up, all attention. Something in the headlong pace of the herd made him uneasy. He scanned the black skyline, trying to discern the still blacker figures of the Chattos who should be riding thereon. But he saw nothing. Once he thought he felt the presence of someone not far from him, and in order to quell the disquietude of his mind he turned his horse up one bank and rode along it for a hundred yards or more. Nothing came of it, except a dangerous stumble on the part of the pony. Still unsatisfied, he dropped back into the gully.

Then, without reason and without tangible evidence of danger, the hair rose at the back of his neck. He slackened his pace and reached for his gun while the horse, a wise, veteran animal, shied away. At almost the same time there came a flash of light and the crack of a gun. The galloping herd vanished in the night and a ringing cry resounded on his right, a cry that was immediately taken up all about him.

The gully seemed to fill with horsemen. The pony stopped dead, quivering in the flanks. A rider came so close to him that a stirrup grazed his leg. And as he sat motionless, mind racing, his ears striving to catch some break in this trap through which he might plunge, he heard a sharp and resounding order issued by a voice that he knew only too well. In response a dozen torches flamed in the darkness and a smell of burning paper and kerosene stung his nostrils. He was trapped.

The furiously blazing torches made a complete ring around him and revealed him as plainly as if he stood in broad daylight. He saw many faces staring grimly at him—faces reflecting the crimson light. These were men he knew. Every last one of them he knew as well as he might have known a brother. Foremost was W. W. Offut, a commanding figure with steely foreboding eyes that seemed to catch flame and burn. Nearby, lolling in the saddle, a dry smile of satisfaction printed on his fat face, was James J. Lestrade. There were other old-time ranch owners in the party, but Lin Ballou had eyes only for those two.

Lestrade could not conceal his pleasure. He said, "Well, I told you boys I'd guarantee results. There's your rustler. Give me credit for having a few sources of information as to what goes on in this country. What do you suppose I travel and make friends for? There's the man you want. Caught cold—and nary a word to say, either."

But Lestrade might have spoken to dumb men as far as results went. Everyone seemed to wait for Offut to speak, and at last he did in a flat, laconic manner.

"Guess we've caught Lin Ballou. Nobody else dragged up in the net, eh?"

"Ain't nobody else," Lestrade declared. "He's the one that did all this thieving."

Offut seemed to weigh this statement. He looked around at the circle of followers and appeared to weigh the possibilities of further search. But the torches were burning low, and if there were other rustlers, they had been given warning enough to put themselves at some distance. So he returned his attention to Lin. The penetrating eyes fell like a blow on the trapped Ballou. Then they seemed to drop a little, as if masking some particular emotion. He spoke again, in the same short, calm manner.

"Your gun, Lin."

Ballou pulled it from the holster, reversed the barrel and handed it over.

"Anything to say? Any confederates to reveal?" Offut asked.

Lin shook his head. In the last spurt of light he saw the cattleman's mouth settle into a thin, compressed smile.

"All right, boys, we'll take him back to Powder and put him in jail. Now, I want you all to understand my judgment on the matter. No talk of lynching. No tolerating the talk from others. I stand for fair trial—always have. Ballou must get it, same as others. Now let's ride."

Ballou turned his horse and came between Lestrade and Offut. Thus guarded, he began the long and dreary march across the mesa and down the slopes to Powder. The party traveled in a straight line, stopping at the Offut ranch for an hour's rest, a meal and fresh horses. Wednesday night, Lin Ballou was locked in the Powder jail.

CHAPTER 7

A STRANGE VISITOR

Confined within the four scarred, bescribbled walls of the jail room on the second floor of the county court-house, Lin Ballou had nothing to do but stare through the grating into the cluttered back area of the building and meditate on the swift turn events had taken. He was not particularly bitter over his situation. That would have been a reversal of his attitude toward life, which was extremely serene and simple. A man's misfortunes, he held, were of his own making and no good ever came of regretting who had been done and could not be recalled. As a man got into trouble, so could he get out. When the tide ran swiftly in one direction it did no good to try to swim against it. The time always came when that tide slackened and reversed itself.

Not that he lacked the spirit to make a good fight. The course of his life proved him a strong and persistent fighter. But he had always understood when to play 'possum and when to spring up and put forth all that there was in him of strength and courage. And according to his belief, the present was a good time to rest and reflect, to wait and see what the authorities meant to do with him.

So he spent Wednesday afternoon whistling the lonely bars of the Cowboy's Lament and that night had a good sound sleep on a bed that was somewhat softer than those in the cave. It was a novelty too, to have the jailer bring his meals on a tray—meals that came from Dick Sharp's Eating Palace across the street and were paid for by the county. The jailer, though a former friend of his, was a man who had the proper cast of mind belonging to his profession. He regarded his captive with a pessimistic, discouraging eye.

"Well, I seen a good many come and go in and outa these portals of justice," he said, opening the door and pushing the breakfast tray through the aperture, "and one and all come to a bad end, soon or late. You can't buck the law, young fellow. They'll get you. Oh, yeah, they'll get you."

"My stomach," Lin said with an air of severity, "doesn't take kindly to cold fodder. See if you can't rush this tray across before the coffee gets a chill."

"You'll guzzle many a cold cup before we're through with you," the jailer said, slamming the door. He pulled at the ends of his walrus-like mustache and squinted between the bars.

"Meaning I'm here for quite a spell? Where's the judge?"

"Off on a fishing trip. Won't be back for a week. Prosecuting attorney along with him. Sheriff, too."

"Well, if the minions of the law can stand it, so can I. My time ain't valuable and the quarters are tolerable.

Only I'm going to ask you not to run any common drunks in with me. I'm a particular prisoner."

The jailer evidently disapproved of this levity. His solemn face settled until it resembled that of a wrinkled and tired bloodhound. "Leave me give you some advice about escaping," he said. "I'm entrusted with you and I'll do my duty. If you try to get out I'll have to use a gun. I'm not a gent to wish for blood—but I see my duty and I'll do it."

"Spoken like a gentleman," Lin said heartily. "Now run along, Rollo, and don't forget about the coffee or I'll put in a complaint to the management."

The jailer retreated down the corridor, closed another door and descended the stairs. Lin ate his meal in peace, built himself a brown-paper cigarette and settled the flat of his back on the bunk. To collect his thoughts he fixed his gaze at a fly speck on the yellow ceiling.

He had been neatly betrayed. That was obvious. The Chattos had done an extra good job and had got themselves out of the way with no difficulty at all. With as little trust as he had in that fine pair of rascals and with all the wariness he had exercised, Lin was forced to admit that they had given him no good grounds for suspicion until the very last moment when the posse had swamped him. Now that it was over he understood the reason for Beauty's lighting the match and the reason for putting him in the rear of the herd. That light had been a signal, perhaps not to the posse as a whole, but at least to some advanced member who had returned to the group and reported it. The Chattos, meanwhile, had quietly dropped away from the gully in the dark and put themselves out of danger.

I might have been a little shrewder, Lin admitted, if I hadn't been so allfired set on discovering something for myself. But seeing that I had a particular job to do,

I let them pull the wool over my eyes. A man naturally wouldn't expect that couple of born crooks to be dickering with a cattle committee. They're not that fond of the law and they know pretty well that the cattlemen don't view them in any favorable light. There's a missing link somewhere.

Somebody who worked with the Chattos had tipped off the committee, and the committee, not knowing that the Chattos were involved, had followed the clue given them.

Such a fellow might be a ranch owner himself, Lin surmised, rolling himself a new smoke. Probably the very same gent who handles their tampered beef for them. Probably some dude in good standing with everybody. Even possibly a member of the cattle committee itself. It's a game where everybody's asking everybody else, "Who's crooked, you or me?" Now, I wonder . . .

He left that particular train of thought to follow another. Why should anyone want to pick on so small and insignificant a creature in the valley's affairs as Lin Ballou? Somebody who had a grudge against him . . .

He sat up and threw away the newly built cigarette. "I've got it," he murmured aloud. "But how am I going to prove it?"

Rising from the bunk, he walked around the room, trying to piece together all the odds and ends of the last forty-eight hours. Noon came, and another good meal from the restaurant, along with the jailer's cheerless presence. And, somewhere beyond the middle of the afternoon, the corridor swung open again and Gracie Henry entered, half running. Valley dust was all over her clothes and trouble was in her eyes. She took one look at Ballou and the cheerless room he had to occupy and then the words tumbled out of her mouth.

"How do they dare do an unjust thing like this? Lin,

78

what made them? Why, when a rider came past our place and told us, I wouldn't believe him at first. What have you done?"

"Didn't the rider tell you?"

"Oh, do you suppose I believe what folks say about you? I don't listen to gossip like that."

The jailer, loitering behind, spoke up. "Well, mebbe it's gossip and mebbe it's truth. When old man Offut catches a man, you can bet your bottom dollar there's a reason."

Gracie Henry was thoroughly angry. She turned on the unfortunate jailer and withered him. "You're an old meddler and you carry tales worse than a woman! Get downstairs and quit spying! I'm not going to carry off your jail."

The jailer suddenly saw his duty to be elsewhere and went to it without argument. Gracie put one hot hand through the grating and touched Lin's shoulder. "Now you look me in the eyes, Lin Ballou, and tell me. Does your conscience tell you you've done something wrong?"

"My conscience," Lin said, smiling just a little at her flushed, half-angry sincerity, "ain't so much of a safe guide as you might reckon. But such as it is, I can truthfully say it doesn't bother me the least."

"Then," Gracie said, "I'll not think another thing about it. Whatever they have against you is wrong. I'm going right over to Dan Rounds—"

Lin shook his head. "You're a fine sport, Gracie girl, but don't do it. I'm asking you not to."

"Why?"

"I'm waiting for folks on the other side of the fence to start the ball rolling. Somebody is mighty interested in seeing me put away and I'm trying to discover who. Let it ride a while."

Gracie came closer to the door and lowered her voice.

79

"Be careful, Lin. I passed three men sitting on the curb below and when they saw me they stopped talking. But one of them had said something about a necktie party."

"Who were they?" Lin asked quickly.

"I don't know them. Some ranch hands."

"I'd certainly like to know which way that wind blows from. Now, Gracie, you better run along. This is no place for a nice girl to be. My love and kisses to the judge."

Serious as she was, that made her smile. "You'd blush to hear his opinion of you now." Her gaze swept the interior of the room. "My, I wish I could get in there with a broom."

"Why, it's right comfortable. I'm having my first rest in several years. Now listen to something, Gracie. It's a treat to have you come, but if I've got it figured right there's certain parties who might make trouble for you. So you stay by the judge until this blows over."

She was a girl with plenty of spirit and the warning did not greatly impress her. But Lin extracted a promise after some persistence. She went down the stairs, gave the jailer another hearty glare and stepped into the street.

The same group of men sat on the curbstone and again fell silent as she passed. One of these, a small, wizened-face creature with watery blue eyes, shot a furtive glance her way and immediately dropped his head. A half block onward, James J. Lestrade stepped out of the grain store and nearly bowed her over. Instantly he was all affability. His hat came off and one pudgy hand fell lightly on her shoulder.

"Gracie, if you're going home let me escort you."

"Thank you," Gracie said shortly. "I've got something else in mind."

Lestrade sobered a little. "Expect you been to see Lin.

Wouldn't do it if I was you, Gracie. Folks are known by the company they keep, you know."

She grew angry again. "I'll not hear a word against him. He's absolutely honest."

Lestrade shrugged his broad shoulders and pursed his lips. "Caught with the goods, Gracie. That's what he was. And it'll go plenty hard with the boy. Well, you tell the judge I'm coming out to see him tonight on a piece of business."

She nodded and passed on. The meeting left her in an extremely unhappy frame of mind. Lestrade's words and manner had carried a threat, both for herself and for Lin Ballou. And his eyes had held an expression she did not like. The man had grown too friendly, too paternal in the past week.

On the opposite side of the street she saw W. W. Offut moving slowly along, seemingly plunged in thought. And although Lin had asked her expressly to forebear appealing to anyone, she acted on impulse and crossed over.

"Mr. Offut," she said, speaking all in a rush, "you're a fair man and you've always been a friend of ours. Now, whatever happens, you've got to see that Lin gets justice. You've *got* to!"

Something like a smile—or the closest approach to it the girl had ever seen—came to the broad, enigmatic face. "Miss Gracie, I'm proud to have you call me fair. Depend on it, the boy will be treated right. Be easy on that. Lin won't lack help."

The manner in which he said it and the way his steel-blue eyes rested on her face comforted her more than anything else could have. Thanking him in a slightly confused manner, she went to her horse and soon was galloping homeward. All the way across the valley she

81

kept hearing Offut's slow, quiet reassurance. There was something powerful in the man.

Meanwhile, Lestrade had sauntered toward his office and busied himself with a sheaf of papers on the desk. Some time afterward the wizened-face ranch hand knocked at the open door and sidled in. He waited for Lestrade to raise his head and then spoke from the corner of his mouth, exactly as a long-term convict would have spoken.

"Boss, I got an idea. Who can tell what friends of this Ballou might slip him? That gal might have given him a hacksaw or a gun."

"Well?"

"There's a window on the second floor of the restaurant building that gives a mighty good view into the jail room. Get me a pair of glasses and I could crawl up there unbeknownst and keep a lookout. Could see if anybody give the kid anything. Wise idea, ain't it?"

"All right, Tracy. You ride to the ranch and get my pair of glasses there. And you'd better have two-three more of the boys drop into town, sort of casual-like."

Tracy hesitated, looked into the street and spoke again, in a still lower tone. "Beauty and Nig Chatto was a-wanting to ride down to town. Said I was to ask you."

Lestrade frowned and toyed with his pencil. He seemed to weigh several things in his mind. "All right, tell 'em to come if they want. But no liquor. And tell 'em I don't want either to even bat an eyelash my way. Trot now. You keep posted around the courthouse when you get back. If anything's attempted you pull the Double Jay boys together and make a fight for it. I don't want any of Ballou's friends to try getting him out. I'll scalp you and every last one of the crew if he does get free. Vamoose."

The man departed. Powder, bereft of the westering

sun, appeared as a town sleeping or abandoned. Then the evening breeze came up and the lamp lights appeared here and there. A piano over in the pool hall began to jangle and from various angles men ambled toward Dick Sharp's Eating Palace to fill the aching void with steak and onions. Thither repaired James J. Lestrade, after which he got his horse from the livery stable and rode out on the Snake River Road, bound for Henry's. The jailer tramped mournfully across the street with Lin Ballou's supper and after a time tramped back again with the empty dishes. The pool hall began to fill, while sundry horsemen rode into town and quietly assembled in the shadows. Most of them seemed to be waiting for something to happen, and from time to time they sauntered by the county courthouse, singly or in pairs.

But nobody saw what was taking place within the Powder Bank. Archer Steele, the cashier, came through the back lots, unlocked the rear door and vanished in the dark vault. Twenty minutes later he slipped out with a bundle under his arm and made a long detour to gain the street at its western end. When he appeared in the restaurant, the bundle had disappeared.

A half-hour later, Steele finished his meal and rode swiftly toward East Flats Junction with a small satchel slung over the pommel. At the junction he unsaddled the horse and turned it loose on the desert. Westward, the long beams of the Limited's headlight shot across the flat land and glistened on the rails. Steele collected a handful of old newspapers from the station shed, spread them between the tracks and made a bonfire to flag the train. The engine roared by and came to a clanking stop. Steele swung up into the vestibule of a sleeper, turned to give a brief farewell glance at the country he had spent the best part of his youth in, and followed the porter inside, the back satchel securely held under his arm.

The action of the cashier had been shrouded in secrecy, but the results burst like a bomb on the sleepy town of Powder next morning, and within four short hours reached the farthest homestead in the valley.

Lin Ballou had finished his breakfast and was chinning himself for exercise on the inner coping of the door when he noticed a man running down the street, shouting at the top of his voice. Lin dropped quickly to the floor and craned his neck to follow this individual on his course. But the corridor intervened between the room and the outer wall of the courthouse, and the window which opened through this wall to allow a view of the street was somewhat higher than the usual window. Therefore, Lin soon lost the man and had to compose himself for further developments.

These were not long in coming.

In three or four minutes the man came back at the same headlong pace, followed by several others, foremost of whom was Lestrade and Dick Sharp of the restaurant. Presently W. W. Offut came into view, walking quite slowly and with his usual dignified air. By now the whole town was turning out. Lin heard the jailer's chair slam against a wall on the lower floor, and shortly, from his limited point of view, he saw that worthy loping after the rest of the crowd.

The center of excitement seemed to be near the bank or Dan Rounds' office. Lin built himself a cigarette, and for want of something better to do, he began to reflect on the excitability of the human family. Here's everybody rushing along as if they were going to a murder, he thought, and I'm burning up because I can't join 'em. If ever there was a time to get out of this bastile, now is it.

He crossed over to the rear window and put his weight against the bars. But he had done this before and decided that it required more strength than he possessed to move them. The courthouse was fairly new and of good design. The former jail had been a thing scandalously easy to depart from, and the authorities, profiting by experience, had contrived to imbed the bars of the new jail room in a cement casement.

The door of the room was itself not a formidable barrier, being like any other door except for the upper half, which had an iron grating; but though the prisoner might possibly pick the lock and get through it, he faced the same kind of cemented and barred windows along the corridor. His only other chance lay in going to the end of the corridor, opening the door and slipping downstairs to the courtroom. Unfortunately, the jailer slept on a cot at the foot of this stairway and during the day sat in a chair from which he commanded a good view in all directions.

Prospects not so good, Lin mused. It's really kind of scandalous to keep a man locked up so tight. Supposing a fire broke out? I'd be in a fine state. However, if a man once got through both of these doors and downstairs without the jailer stopping him, he could make a run for the rear of the courtroom and into the judge's chamber. It's just a step, then, to the back alley and the open air. Humm. Worse jails have been busted. . . . I think Sourface is coming back.

The jailer, in common with the general run of men, had news and desired to spread it. He bowled down the corridor and put a perspiring face up to the grating.

"By God, there's sure trouble afoot now. Know what's been done? There's something like fifty-nine thousand

85

dollars stole from the bank and Archer Steele plumb gone from these parts. His horse come a-roaming home a spell back, minus gear. Old Elathan Boggs opened the bank and found everything missing."

"All gone?" Lin asked incredulously.

"No, not everything," the jailer qualified. "Old Boggs, he never trusts nobody with bank money. Keeps the vault combination to himself. But Steele had the water project funds in another part. Every red cent of *that* is gone!"

Lin shut his mouth tightly, and there passed across his mind the picture of Hank Colqueen, broiled red by the hot sun, tugging at his stubborn fence wire, fighting tooth and toenail to scratch a living from a barren land. Hank had five hundred dollars in that water fund. It was a vivid picture and equally true of better than a hundred other families likewise hard hit by the misfortune. That money was not surplus savings; it was their very substance and represented almost the full mortgage value of the land. Something stuck in Lin Ballou's throat and his whole body grew hot with rage.

"If it's Steele that got the money I hope they hang him!"

"Oh, we'll get him," the jailer said hopefully. "Nobody can buck the law, young fellow. Some dudes get smart and think they can, but it ain't possible." He returned downstairs, locking the corridor door behind him.

It's happened too blamed soon to seem like a matter of Providence, Lin thought. First a supply house burns down, then a ditch digger lies idle. Now it's embezzling. If Steele's crooked, it sure looks bad for all these poor folks with their capital tied up in the affair. It's plumb impossible for them to raise that sum again. Not more than a thousand dollars cash left in the whole valley, I'll bet. They've got to head off that fifty-nine thousand.

But there was no such encouraging news as the morning wore on. Instead, the town began to fill up with settlers, men of all ages and all types, but terribly alike in their soberness. Most of them carried guns, and their first move after tying their horses and teams was to march down the street, past the courthouse, to the bank and Lestrade's office. Lin watched them come and keep coming until the street was choked with vehicles, beasts and men. Sounds of speechmaking rose from time to time, the words too faint for Lin to hear, but seeming to issue from the same man each time. Lin made a guess that it was Lestrade.

A hot day's work cut out for him, and no mistake, he thought sourly.

But during the afternoon there arrived in town a pair of riders who made Lin Ballou lose all interest in the irrigation affair. They were much alike, both swarthy and roving-eyed. They, too, carried guns and sat in their saddles as if expecting trouble. As they rode by the courthouse they lifted their glances along the second story and at that moment Ballou saw them. Their very audacity took the breath from him until he recollected that the sole witness of their outlawry was himself.

Beauty and Nig, proud as life, he thought. What brought *them* in? When the buzzards begin to collect it's sure high time to watch out. Lin, old boy, something tells me your skin is entirely unsafe.

Again his reflections were interrupted by the opening of the corridor door. The jailer's voice rose in querulous protest. "I can't be allowing every doggoned soul in Powder to see Ballou. I don't know as I ought to let you in."

Lin heard Dan Rounds issue a flat challenge. "Trying to keep men *incommunicado?*"

That was a poser. The jailer didn't know what *incom-*

municado meant and he sullenly stated the fact. "But I know my duty," he said.

"Well, you don't know law," Rounds said brusquely. "I have the right to see any prisoner in this jail and if you deny me that right I'll make a report and you'll lose your job." His slim, somewhat cynical face appeared before the grating, much to Ballou's pleasure. "By golly, here's one honest man to visit my premises," Ballou exclaimed. "Dan, if you've come to offer legal advice—"

"Legal advice!" the lawyer snorted. "What good is that in a county that doesn't know Blackstone from Doctor Whu's bitter-root almanac?" He swung on the jailer who stood with his chin within a foot of the cell door. "What are you snooping around here for? Get back to the end of the corridor and stay there!"

"I know my duty—"

Rounds cut him off impatiently. "If you interfere with my privileges again I'll put a contempt charge against you. Vamoose!" He watched the jailer slowly retreat, at the same time winking to Lin. The jailer slammed the corridor door and announced as he descended the stairs, "I'm a-going to see about this when the judge gets back."

"*When* he gets back," Rounds retorted. His belligerence fell from him, and he dropped his voice. "Lin, my boy, you don't need legal advice. That's a feeble prop under the circumstances. What you need is something to get you out of here in a hurry."

"That bad?" Lin said.

The lawyer's eyes clouded. "I know more about crooked politics than you do, *amigo mio*. And I can read the signs of the hour pretty clearly. Damn them!"

"What's got you so steamed up?"

The lawyer smiled in a sad, wistful manner. "I hate to see a man—any man—railroaded. If I was just free—" He checked himself and shook his head. For quite some time he was silent, watching Ballou as if attempting to find words to express what he felt. "Been friends for a mighty long spell, haven't we?"

"Something," Lin said, "is sure under your skin."

"More than you know. Listen, old boy, I know what they've charged you with and I know Offut's the man who brought you in. But that doesn't make you crooked. You can't be crooked. It just isn't in you. Oh, I'm not denying that there's plenty of crookedness in the world —and you'd be surprised if you knew just who-all had a hand in the grafting going on right now—but you're as straight as a string. I'd stake my left hand on it."

Ballou felt a little embarrassed. "Run that heifer into the pen," he said.

"I wish," Rounds said, toying with his watch charm, "I could make a fight for you. But—" Here his words died. For a lawyer he found it difficult to say what he wished. "Point is, I've got to make a trip to Portland right away. Try to arrange for—for something to tide the irrigation affairs over." He looked down the corridor and crowded his body up to the cell door. His hand went into his coat and came out with a revolver, butt first. He passed it through the grating. "Take it, kid, and hide it."

Lin's hand gripped the gun. It vanished. "I feel a sight better right now," he admitted.

Rounds stepped away, a half smile on his face, the hazel eyes moving strangely. He put his hand through the bars. "You won't see me again for a spell. So long, Lin. Remember me in your prayers."

Lin gripped the slim, aristocratic hand. Rounds walked quickly down the hall and the door closed behind him.

The long and turbulent afternoon drew to a close. Powder began to resume its normal quietude, with the settlers driving away one by one. But Lin, watching the small vista of the street in front, noticed more cowpunchers than usual floating slowly back and forth. That would have given him no particular cause for speculation had he not discovered another fact. Most of these men were from the Double Jay, James J. Lestrade's outfit.

Where there's a smoke there's got to be a fire, he thought. It's high time I did something. Let's see, now. I've got a gun, and that changes the caged canary's warble a little. It's about three jumps to the back end of the livery stable. Once I sifted out of here I might be able to lift a horse from its stall without too much attention. Well, I ought to be able to tie old Sourface in a knot, first off. That's not going to be hard. Same with the stable hand, if there's only one hanging around. Time enough to get away in, when dark comes. Then what? No use breaking jail unless . . .

He sat on his bunk and rolled one cigarette after another, worrying the problem around in his mind. Dusk fell and the jailer brought his supper. Some time later the man came back for the tray and issued a lugubrious statement. "The law's a powerful instrument, young fellow. But sometimes there's a miscarriage of justice. All I got to say is, I wish I didn't have such a doggoned big responsibility. If trouble comes I ain't going to risk my skin for a cattle rustler." With which he slid away, slamming the corridor door behind him more vigorously than usual.

Another indication of how the wind blows, Ballou decided. All right, I'll get going.

But other actors were moving about in the darkened streets of Powder. Before Lin Ballou could make his move, another man quietly and secretly sent a messenger to draw the jailer away from the courthouse. That accomplishment behind him, he slipped into the back door of the courtroom and started upstairs to the cell.

CHAPTER 8

THE KILLING

Lin Ballou had heard the jailer's voice rise in a protest and a little later he saw the man, accompanied by another, cross the street and stand for an instant in the light shining out of Sharp's restaurant. Hardly had the pair vanished when he was aware of a sound in the courtroom below. A heavy body came slowly up the stairs. The corridor door stood fast under an exploring arm, and then the lock turned and the intruder advanced down the hall. Ballou drew his gun and stepped into the darkest corner of the cell, waiting for trouble. But when a massive pair of shoulders appeared before the grating and a great head stooped a little to peer in —outlined faintly by the dim light coming through the corridor window—he dropped the point of the gun and moved quickly to the door. W. W. Offut's voice summoned him.

"Lin, you step close where I can talk."

Ballou made a protest. "You shouldn't have come, Mr. Offut. If anybody sees you it'll be a dead giveaway."

"Things are narrowing to a point," the cattleman

replied. "Had to do it. I made a turn through the back of the building into the rear door. Don't think I was watched. If I was it doesn't cut such a figure, at this stage of the game. You've got to make a break for it."

"Trouble?"

"Lot of Double Jay boys on the street and a few other ranch hands. Smell trouble. Best you should get out of the way before they try something. I wouldn't want to have to rescue you before the crowd and reveal the true situation. We're not ready for it yet—unless you discovered something in the mesa. Did you?"

Lin did not answer this directly, but asked a question of his own. "Who put you up to making the raid?"

"Jim Lestrade. He certainly slid it over on me. I didn't have any idea I was going to trap you, and he wouldn't say who gave him the information. Guess maybe he was just taken in by appearances."

"No he wasn't," Ballou said. "That was a deliberate move of his. I can't prove it, Mr. Offut, but I'm willing to take oath he's the man you and I and the rest of the committee are trying to uncover."

Offut turned the information over in his mind and ended by saying mildly, "That's a serious charge, Lin. What makes you think it?"

"Listen. I deliberately put myself in the way of being seen the other day. You know I've been trying to get somebody to swallow that hook for a month. Well, the Chattos bit. Made an offer for me to join 'em. I did." He leaned forward, waggling his finger to stress his information. "When you corraled me the Chattos got away clear. Why did they get away clear? Because they meant to have me fall in the trap alone. Beauty even lit a cigarette as a sort of signal—"

"I saw that," Offut interposed. "Mighty careless, I thought."

"Careless, nothing. It was a part of their plan. By the time you men closed in they'd ridden a mile off. That's why you didn't catch 'em. Now they couldn't have done that unless somebody in the valley had made all the arrangements. Who made those arrangements? Figure it for yourself."

"Jim Lestrade," Offut said.

"Sure. Those cattle we were hazing down the gully had been cut out by Nig and Beauty before dark. They wouldn't tell me what brand they meant to slap on or anything about the agent that took the critters and shipped 'em. But they did say there was an agent who got fifty per cent of the profit for doing that little act of charity. Isn't it pretty clear who that particular man is?"

Offut sighed. "Somehow I had a suspicion it was a neighbor of mine—but I didn't reckon it would hit so close to home as Jim Lestrade." After a long interval he spoke in a cold, brusque manner. "Well, I've had to hang neighbors of mine before this—men I thought mighty good friends. Guess I can do it again. But we can't do anything without evidence. I will not lynch. We've got to get facts a jury can understand. They didn't let you in on anything, did they?"

"The Chattos are mighty clever. If I could have got hold of some branding irons, or if I'd been left alone until they started blotting out the old marks, I could have had something definite."

"Just can't see why either the Chattos or Lestrade should want you out of the road," Offut said.

"I've been thinking about that. It's either because they wanted to get somebody to take all the blame for rustling and thereby leave the land free for themselves again, or else it's because Lestrade knows I'm against his water project. Might be either, and sometimes I think it's a little of both."

A crowd of men passed beneath the courthouse, raising their voices. Ballou stirred. "You'd better make tracks."

"You've got to get evidence," Offut said.

"Well, I've made up my mind to try some rough work. I'll bring you in two good pieces of evidence, once I part company with this bastile."

Offut's hand slipped through the grating. "Here's a key. I've had one of the boys lead the jailer off on a wild goose chase. They'll hold him for half an hour. There's a horse saddled and waiting, with a gun and belt full of cartridges hanging on the horn. It's behind the livery stable. Ten minutes after I leave, you unlock the doors and go out the back way. I can't tip my own hand too much in this right at present, but I've got three safe, close-mouthed men stationed in the shadows to cover your break, just in case there's any opposition. If you want a posse to back you up in the mesa, tell me so."

"No, that would scare the Chattos clear out of the state. But I'll ask that you have your men strung around town three-four days from now when I come riding in with my evidence. There may be opposition from the Double Jay boys."

"All right," Offut said, and Lin Ballou felt the man's eyes boring through the darkness. "Lin, I'm sorry I've had to make it seem like I mistrusted you. Folks all think you're no account. That's been hard on you and maybe lost you friends, temporarily. Just consider it necessary. A man's got to do a lot of disagreeable work in this world to chase out the crooks. Guess I've lost more sleep on that score than you."

"We'll call it even," Lin said, embarrassed.

"You'll not lose from it," Offut said in that definite, reassuring manner of his.

Without more comment he slid down the hallway,

closed the last door and locked it—a protection against any possible return of the jailer or of Double Jay men trying to force the place in the intervening minutes—and let himself out the rear entrance of the court room. For so large a man, he moved very quietly through the piles of boxes and broken wagon beds, and he took an alley that led him once more to the street. Stepping into the semilighted thoroughfare he suddenly brushed the side of a man loitering nearby. He drew up sharply. A powerful arm shot out and gripped the loiterer's arm with such force as to make the man wince.

"What are you doing here, sir?" Offut demanded. Swinging him about until a ray of light fell on his face, he saw it to be Tracy of the Double Jay.

"Beg your pardon, sir," Tracy said, squirming. "Didn't mean to hit you. But it's a free street, ain't it?"

"I dislike being crowded by drunks," Offut said.

"Thought you were one of them. Very sorry." He walked on.

Tracy waited until Offut had vanished, then cut across the street and through a back lot. In his speed he grew careless and struck a piece of barbwire that sent him sprawling into a pile of trash. The pain of that accident made him curse violently, but without delay he got up and went on, to come at last to the rear door of James J. Lestrade's office.

Five or six Double Jay men were standing there in the darkness, silent and formidable. One challenged him and lighted a match to identify him. Knocking on the door, he went in to face his boss.

"Well, here's a piece of news for you," he announced triumphantly. "I'm watching from the second story again and I see a shadow through the jail window that I can't make out. So I go down to the street and wait by the nearest alley entrance. And who do you suppose comes out of it?"

Lestrade motioned for the man to go on.

"W. W. Offut! He's been up to see Ballou. That's why the jailer was took off on a visit."

The force of that man's name and all that it stood for was enough to bring Lestrade out of his chair. The jovial face grew perceptibly whiter and the thick jowels seemed to sag. His first move was to stride over to the lamp and turn down the wick.

"Offut. Offut. What's that mean? My God, is he playing a game with all of us? Have we got ourselves hooked up on the wrong line? Tracy, you back out of here. If Offut's got a hand in it there's something wrong. Spread the boys around town. Post some of them back of the jail. Put another at each street end. If it's to be a try at getting loose, I'll have something to say. Watch sharp, now! If Ballou puts his head outside of that place knock him over! Somebody's got wind of what we aimed to do. Knock him over, I'm telling you. Get out of here!"

Tracy departed, gathering up the Double Jay men as he went.

Lestrade mopped a handkerchief over his face, which glistened with fine beads of sweat. He did not lack physical courage, but he understood too well the driving strength of W. W. Offut. That man stood like a beacon in the affairs of the valley. His lifelong code had been honesty. Throughout the state he was known as one who, once embarked on the trail of an outlaw, never took a backward step. There was something quite grim and terrible about the inflexibility of his will that pierced even the toughest hides.

They can't prove anything on me, he thought, staring through the dark room. Not so long as the Chattos keep their mouths shut. And they won't do anything else unless

96

they figure to hang themselves. As for Ballou, he can't prove a thing, even though he knows the Chattos and me are neck and neck, which I doubt. But for safety's sake we'll have to take care of him. If he don't break, we'll have to finish the lynching job we started. Now, in regards to Mr. Dan Rounds . . .

He took his revolver out of the desk drawer and thrust it into the holster, after which he buckled on the belt. The inquisitive Tracy, watching from his vantage point earlier in the afternoon, had seen the lawyer's arm carry something through the grating to Lin Ballou. This fact, when reported to Lestrade, only strengthened the cattleman's belief in the uncertain mind of the lawyer. He had judged Rounds, some time before, as one who was not quite dishonest enough to be trusted.

Rounds meant to betray him, he knew. And there was one witness he couldn't let live.

He stepped from his office under the cloak of darkness and crossed the street. Considering the affair from all angles, he decided he had not been fortunate in the choice of his confederates. Steele had double-crossed him too, running off with the project's money, although Lestrade knew that this defalcation really aided his scheme. It broke the settlers that much sooner and it placed the blame on the shoulders of another than his own. Nevertheless, he had been betrayed, and the settlers, as they came into town, had linked him with Steele in their accusations. Decidedly, times were getting dangerous.

"We've got just a few chores to do before we pull freight," he muttered, looking across the way to Dan Rounds' office.

The light therein burned brightly, and he saw the lawyer seated at the table, writing rapidly. He was a fair mark for any gun. Lestrade, concealed by the shadows, leaned against a building and took preliminary aim with his revolver. Satisfied, he dropped the weapon and waited.

Lin Ballou judged the minutes as they sagged by, listening for the possible return of the jailer or some chance townsman straying into the courthouse. Dick Sharp's restaurant emitted its fitful lights through a window that was fogged with steam. Across this vista men passed and passed again, moving with a carelessness that did not fool him. It seemed that in the time elapsing after Offut's departure there was a greater movement among those cowpunchers. Once he thought he heard the boards below creak, and he laid his ear against the grating and listened.

The ten minutes, he decided, were up. Turning the key in the lock, he opened the door and slipped down the corridor. After passing the second barrier, he stopped for an instant to fix in his mind the path out of the building and across the rear area to the stable. The foot of the stairway was nothing but a wall of mystery, ink-black. Descending on his toes, he raised the revolver and moved it slowly from side to side.

A board groaned beneath his weight. Farther down he thought he heard someone move within the courtroom. But he had no time to stop and explore all these strange sounds. His imagination created most of them, anyway. Time pressed. At the bottom of the stairs he turned, opened the swinging doors of the courtroom and threaded his way between the benches to the rostrum. To the left was the exit into the back lot, which, when he put a hand to the knob, he discovered to be swinging ajar. On the threshold he paused again.

The little world of Powder seemed to revolve slowly in the night, the usual sounds and the usual smells permeating the air. It was so quiet that he distinctly heard the clatter of the Chinese dishwasher in the restaurant across the street. The pool hall piano sent forth its off-key harmony. On the left, a thin shaft of light came through a crack of Stagg's store, wherein the grocery man waited for the last penny's trade of the day. To the right was another wall, devoid of windows. Between these, Lin Ballou set forth, careful not to step into any pile of rubbish or knock over any stray box. Muscle and nerve and hearing—all were at that high pitch which serves a man in danger or emergency.

He reached the end of this lot safely and rounded the corner of Stagg's store. Just beyond was the stable, and there, according to Offut, a horse and saddle waited in readiness. It was a clear path as Ballou remembered it, so he moved faster. Suddenly a shadow appeared before him, the shadow of his posted animal. A body rose straight up from the ground and put forth an arm.

Reins fell in his hand and a voice whispered, "Don't fiddle. Make a bust for it. There's somebody waiting behind that shed."

He swung into the saddle, strapped the revolver belt around him and dug in the spurs. The horse shot away. The flight was on.

The first sound of hoofs brought another answer. From the shed, from the stable roof and from some other covert, poured a volley of fire. He saw a long orange finger of flame sear the shadows beside him and heard the solid plunk of a bullet in the stable wall. Ten yards farther, a body ran beside him and seemed to reach for the horse's head. His revolver slashed down and struck solid bone. He felt a man clutch his leg, then fall against the rump of the horse. A scream rose above the gunfire, evoking a still greater hail of lead.

Fearing that they would bring down his horse, Lin Ballou kicked his feet from the stirrups and bent very low. He shot past another alley, catching a momentary view of lantern light bobbing in the street. Behind him, other guns joined the argument, and for a moment the bullets fell away from him and took another target. At this, he knew that Offut's men were distracting the Double Jay fire. Reassured, he fled onward, left the protection of the buildings and cut directly across the eastern end of Powder's only street. Glancing down this thoroughfare, he saw many men running in one direction and another, crossing the beams of light from the restaurant, Stagg's store and, lastly, from Dan Rounds' office.

As he watched, he heard another gun fire nearby. Glass splintered and then a heavy body appeared in the outthrown lamp rays of the lawyer's office. There was a final burst of guns, and after that silence descended over the town. Many lanterns began to swing through the darkness. Somebody began to shout. The street filled with running men. All seemed to be rushing in the direction of the livery stable.

Lin Ballou veered to the northeast on the road and spoke to the horse. "Steady now, boy. Settle down and stretch your legs. It's a long trip you've got to make."

The town and its excitement drifted behind him. The cool desert air ran by his body and the aromatic smell of sage was in his nostrils. Far away, the mesa bulked against the black velvet skyline.

The Chattos are probably still in town, he mused, but they won't be so very long. I judge that there'll be a general posse after me in five or ten minutes and if they aren't in that posse, they'll at least be making a run for the mesa. I'll find them in their old stamping grounds soon enough.

The posse was indeed getting under way within the time he guessed. But before the posse departed from town a final scene had to be acted out, unknown to Ballou. The splintering of glass he had heard was caused by a bullet passing through Dan Rounds' office window. The bullet ended its journey in the lawyer's chest. It had not killed him outright, for when Offut, Lestrade and several others reached him, he was bent over in the chair, pressing one hand against the slowly trickling blood.

Offut took hold of the lawyer's shoulder and pulled him upright. "Dan—Dan, do you hear me, boy? Who did this?"

The lawyer summoned the last fading breath of his life. He raised his head until he looked squarely into the face of James J. Lestrade. He smiled in his tired, cynical manner.

"What difference does it make?" he muttered, and died.

CHAPTER 9

THE FIGHT IN THE DARK

The posse kept hard on his trail as he swept across that undulating sea of sand. Twice he spent a precious minute to stop and put an ear to the ground. Each time the faint throbbing of hoofs was borne through the earth to him and each time he swung to the saddle and changed his direction. The moon was young—a thin pale crescent that suffused the world with a dim silver glow. Under it sage and juniper were transformed into mysterious, fantastic shapes and the horizon on all sides of him seemed to march off to infinity. The night wind cooled him. Afar, a coyote sent forth its quivering challenge. He felt the rhythmic swell of the pony's muscles and the steady onward thudding of the pony's feet. This animal had been carefully chosen for tonight's work. It seemed to know what it had to do and where it had to go. The long, sleek head stretched well forward, pointing like a compass needle toward the mesa.

This race would not be to the swift. That Lin Ballou well understood. In the darkness he had the advantage. They could not follow his tracks, nor could they be sure which way he traveled. But that posses would be composed almost wholly of Double Jay men and more than probably the Chattos would also be along. The Chattos well knew his stamping ground and could guess too easily where he would try to hide. Therefore, as long as he kept his present course they were pretty certain to be on the right trail. It behooved him to change his methods and resort to subterfuge.

As a matter of fact, he did not want to throw the posse completely off the scent. As he rode he began to build certain plans that just might work out, with a fair degree of luck. They might take him as far as the mesa, or they might bring him to a stand a great deal short of that point. Anyhow, the less riding he had to do the better it would be and the less trouble he would have in getting back to town.

The thing for me to do, he decided, is to swing off and double back until I get in the rear of that bunch of thieves. They'll never suspect me of trailing them. Which is exactly the right course for me to follow. I can't accomplish much until I know how many's in that gang.

102

If they should split up in bunches I might get some-where.

On he went. To the right of him, a quarter mile, he saw the glimmer of W. W. Offut's ranch lights. Another hour of this steady gait passed and he swung to miss Lestrade's home fences. Still onward he proceeded until he saw, looming up in the dark like a misshapen ghost of the desert, the old, abandoned Twenty Mile homestead shacks. The land here began to swell and fall in sharper, more abrupt folds, affording him a greater measure of protection. Going fifty yards beyond the shanty he stopped the pony in a convenient hollow and left it. Then he climbed up to a commanding piece of ground and lay flat on his stomach.

The faint reverberation rose to a distinct thrumming and then died away entirely. In the silver gray shadows he saw three horesmen walking their animals around the corner of the shanty. The rest of the posse was nowhere to be seen or heard. At some point back on the trail they had turned off. The trio in front of him stopped. Two of them dismounted and seemed to hold a parley. Ballou could hear the rise and fall of their speech, but nothing else. A match flared and made a short, gleaming curve upward. By that instant's light he recognized the man in the saddle.

Lestrade.

He crawled forward, maneuvering so that he presently had the shack between him and the three. This accomplished, he rose and boldly walked forward until he stood in the protection of a wall. As he arrived, he heard Beauty Chatto's voice rumbling along, irate and threatening.

"Fine mess, ain't it? Long as this yahoo's floating free around these parts you and us has got trouble a-plenty and no mistake. What was all the delay about? You had him right where you wanted him. Why didn't you organize a necktie bee and yank him out of jail?"

"Violence," Lestrade responded, "ain't the best policy unless a man's got to come to it. Any jury would have took care of him proper. Even so, I did have it all planned to have the boys pull him out and get rid of him. But there was a little accident. I don't know exactly what Offut's got to do with Lin Ballou, but he's the man that helped him get away."

"Well, if old man Offut's stringing along with Ballou, you can bet your neck Ballou is exactly what I thought he was in the first place. A spy of the committee's. I wish I'd kept that hunch. Instead, he plays me for a sucker and I bite. Then you arrange that damnfool idea, and now we're all in a jackpot. Why, say, Nig and me is liable to get picked off the minute we put a foot in the mesa. Fine fix, ain't it?"

"He's got to be stopped," Lestrade announced decisively.

"Well, why didn't you stop him when you had it in your hands?" Beauty demanded, more and more belligerent.

"Hold onto yourself," Lestrade countered coldly. "If you boys won't do it, I'll go and fetch the crew from the ranch and we'll get a whole posse on his tracks again."

"Now," Chatto growled, "that ain't a bright idea either. You know nothing about trailing. Want to scare him clean across the state line? Nig and me knows where he holes in. We'll get him. But just bear in mind that we won't fiddle around. We'll get him cold. That'll be an end of the trouble. If you'd give me the office to put him away in the first place all this'd been avoided. The trouble is, you want Ballou killed but you ain't never had the gizzard to come out and say so."

"I don't know as I'll take that, Beauty," Lestrade said, turning in the saddle. "Keep your talk to yourself."

"Keep hell!" Beauty retorted. "I'll talk how I please. You better sing low to me."

"Yes, Listen, my friend, I can put you where you'll have a long time to think about your words."

Beauty's body swayed forward. "Don't you threaten *me!* I got a few secrets I could tell myself."

"Secrets!" Lestrade cried. "Why, you fool, do you think I'm a man to leave evidence against me in the hands of such scum as you? Oh, no! There's not a single scrap of paper or a single pen mark you've got to bind me with."

"Huh. There's other things besides paper. If Nig and me was ever caught we'd turn evidence. Two witnesses is enough to tie you in a knot. But I've had you figured as a double-crosser for a long spell. What about the brand irons that's hid away up by the six pines? And here's something else: Your foreman knows how many cows you shipped each time. I know how many I added to the East Flats pens each time. The stockyard man at Portland knows how many you sold him. Well, if it comes to a showdown, these things could be checked up by the cattle committee. That foreman of yours is a squealer for certain. He'd cross his grandma if he thought it'd save his hide."

"Figured it out to a fraction, didn't you," Lestrade said. "Well, Beauty, you'll never squeal. It means your neck if you do."

"No more will you," Beauty said. "I'm just showing you where to head in. Don't try to hush me."

Nig, who seldom spoke, broke in at this point to act as peacemaker. " 'Tain't no time for a quarrel. We got a job to do."

"Right," Lestrade said, turning to his horse. "Get it

done. I'll see you boys taken care of. But don't come to town in company with any of the Double Jay outfit. I got to warn you on that." He started away.

Beauty had not yet got the whole of his grievance stated and he moved into the night, one hand on Lestrade's stirrup. "There's another matter I want to—" His words were lost as he strode off. Nig, as if fearful of trouble, followed.

Here was the golden opportunity Lin Ballou wished for. Slipping around the shanty, he stepped through the open door and into the ink-black room. He knew his way perfectly in these quarters, for he had spent many nights under the shelter of the battered, half-caved-in roof. To itinerant travelers or ranch hands bent on long journeys, it was a well known refuge when darkness found them short of their destination. Built many years ago by a homesteader with more courage than resources, it had been soon abandoned to its fate—a single-room stopover shelter with a few rough pieces of furniture, two bunks and an old cast-iron stove.

Once upon a time there had been an attic, but wayfarers in want of fuel had stripped most of the boards away from the rafters. A few still remained, however, and Lin, casting about for a means of hiding himself, struck upon this place as the best. He found a chair and stood on it, at the same time gripping a rafter. Swinging upward, he crawled over to a corner of the place and lay flat on the boards. It was concealment, but not much more.

He had no more than reached this vantage point when he heard the Chatto brothers moving back into the shanty, talking. One of them came cautiously through the door, silhouetted against the gray shadows.

"You suppose we can light up?" queried a voice which he recognized as Nig's.

Beauty, unsaddling the horses, thought it was safe enough and said so. "Lin, he's ten miles east of here by now. That boy likes the mesa. We'll follow his tracks in the morning till we hit rock. After that I got a good idea."

"You're always full of ideas," Nig muttered. He was the milder and more practical of the two. Standing directly under Ballou, he lit a match and applied it to the wick of a lamp that from time to time had been supplied with kerosene by thoughtful ranch hands. The dim rays flared out, doing little more than cast the upper half of the shanty into a still blacker gloom. Beauty tramped in with the gear and threw it on the floor.

"Light a fire, Nig. It's getting chilly."

"What with? Ain't nothing to burn unless we take the table."

Beauty raised his eyes toward the few remaining attic boards and Lin saw the dark, surly face explore the reaches of his hiding place. But the lamp light's glare blinded the man for the time. Moving forward, he stretched his arm, trying to reach the rafters.

"We'll bring down one of them boards."

"Too much trouble," Nig said. "Roll up in your blanket. We got to get a night's sleep if we aim to travel hard in tho morning."

Beauty changed his mind and planted himself on a bunk. "That Lestrade jasper better not pull anything on me. I'll take a shot at him. Sometimes I think it'd be a damn good idea. His head's too full of schemes. Nig, he'd sell you or me for a plugged nickel if he thought it'd help him."

Nig was not without a certain impartiality. "So'd you and me sell him if it'd help us. It don't do for us to fall out with him. Means money. You always got a chip on your shoulder lately. What's eating you?"

107

Beauty took off his gunbelt and draped it over the corner of his bunk, making sure that the butt of the weapon was within easy reach. Removing his boots, he wrapped himself as tightly as he could in the saddle blanket and settled himself at full length on the bunk.

"I tell you, Nig, this country is sure getting civilized. 'Tain't no place for you and me any more. I been feeling it in my bones there's going to be a big bust pretty soon. Know why? I'll tell you. When W. W. Offut gets to dickering with gents like Ballou it means there's something wrong. Ballou knows about us. He's prob'ly told Offut. I ain't anxious to attract Offut's attention, nohow."

"I'd as lief tackle a nest of snakes myself," Nig confessed.

Beauty raised himself on an elbow, face settling in brutal lines. "First we're going to drill Ballou. Then we move to new range. If it should happen you and me is lassoed before we move, then I swear I'll put a bullet through Lestrade somehow."

Lin gripped his revolver and with infinite care raised himself inch by inch. He had full view of Beauty, but Nig was out of his vision, still near the stove. As he moved, Nig crossed over to the door and closed it, belt in one arm and a boot in the other. At that moment Lin stood on his knees and threw down the muzzle of his gun, issuing a sharp metallic warning.

"Stay put, both of you! Don't move an inch! Nig—drop that belt!"

Nig obeyed instantly, his body assuming the rigidity of a statue. But Beauty was of tougher disposition. In a flash he had rolled from the bunk, hand yanking the gun from its holster. He struck the floor with a resounding thud and tried to bring his weapon into play. But the blanket he had wrapped himself in was his undoing.

Ballou sent a bullet within a foot of the broad easy mark on the floor.

"Steady now, or I'll let you have it. Drag that hand away. That's the boy. Seeing as you're so good at rolling, just roll right on toward the door. Uh-huh. Keep going, Beauty. Now stand up beside your handsome brother."

Lin dropped out of the attic and scooped Beauty's weapon from the floor. "Now both of you slide around toward the stove."

Beauty's face was a battleground of emotion. His thin lips drew back from long, yellow teeth and his eyes were wide and flaring. "You can't get away with it," he challenged. "You can't handle me and Nig. Better clear out peaceful before we kill you."

"Always making a bluff of it, eh, Beauty? Don't you know me better than that? I don't scare easy. Now cut out that fiddling with your hands. Step around toward the stove. Lift your feet! I want you alive, amigo, but if I can't take you that way I'll shoot you dead."

Nig moved docilely, but Beauty's every motion was a protest. He scowled with each step, stopped to curse his captor and had to be prompted with the gun muzzle before he'd move again. The wide, bold eyes raced around the room as if seeking a way to challenge Ballou's attention. He stared at the rafters and squinted shrewdly at the smoky lamp on the table. It was plain to see that he had set his mind against being taken. Ballou watched him closely. There was no more dangerous character in the breadth and length of the valley than this ugly, stubborn Chatto. Suddenly the man's swart face broke into a grin and he looked past Ballou to the door.

"Well, that's the time I foxed you. Thought you'd get me, eh? Old Beauty's too slick. There's a gun pointed at the middle of your back. Come in, Jake."

Ballou resisted a powerful urge to turn his head. The

door seemed to creak behind him. The following moment was long as eternity. Nothing came of it. No voice commanded him to drop his gun. He summoned a grin of his own.

"That's an old trick, amigo. I cut my eyeteeth on it. Now, are you going to herd up to the stove or ain't you?"

Beauty's face mirrored a disappointed rage. The man fought every inch of the way, summoning all the guile of his nature, recalling all the old tricks he had learned. Within arm's reach of the table he stopped and issued another threat. "I ain't going to be took, Lin. That's flat. You can't kill me because you ain't got nothing against me. There's a murder charge staring you in the face if you pull that trigger. Who'd listen to the excuses of a cattle rustler? No, you can't do it."

"No? Use your memory, Beauty. When did I ever say anything I didn't back up? What I said about taking you is gospel truth. As for murder, I'll chance it. Either Lin Ballou's the goat or else the Chattos are. I can tell you now it's not going to be me. Sit down in that chair, Beauty, I aim to tie you with your own rope. Careful now."

He slid aside somewhat to reach for Chatto's lariat on the floor. As he stooped he saw the big man rub his palm against the side of his shirt and wipe the sweat from his face.

A glance passed between the brothers—a glance so significant that Ballou straightened without getting the rope.

"Careful, boys," he warned.

Nig moved from the stove with a short, jerky motion and at the same time emitted a loud bellow. As Lin looked his way Beauty struck the table with his arm, and sent it crashing on its side. The lamp chimney broke into a thousand pieces and there was a great flare of light, followed by darkness. By that momentary flare Ballou saw Beauty Chatto's great body leaping toward him.

He did not want to kill the man. Beauty was worth a lot more as a living witness than as a dead body. So, as he sent a shot crashing through the shadows, he aimed somewhat aside from the mark, hoping to wing his captive and stop the rush. He knew he had aimed well, for he heard a sound that was half a grunt and half a cry. Then he was struck with a terrible force and sent back against the wall of the shanty so hard that every board in the place rattled. It knocked the wind completely from his body. In that moment he was completely paralyzed, sick from head to feet and straining to breathe. There was not an ounce of strength in him.

A fist crashed into his face and an arm wrenched the gun from his right hand. He was thrown to the floor with Beauty atop him. A knee plunged into his chest, and as he rolled aside the butt of Beauty's weapon splintered the boards where his head had been a moment before. In the daze of half consciousness he heard the big man laboring out oath after oath. Beauty's breath poured into his face. Nig's feet seemed to stumble back and forth at the far end of the room, not venturing closer.

He had fended as best he could with weak, ineffectual elbows. Presently his breath came back on a tide of reviving strength. In his left hand he still held another gun—the one he had taken from Beauty's bunk. The upper half of the arm was pinioned, but he threw all of his weight into a rolling move and freed himself, aiming a blow across the darkness that struck Beauty along the cheek. A desperate fury hardened his muscles. Raising his legs, he sent Beauty off balance, rolled and got the man clear of his body.

There was an instant of deceptive quiet, followed by

a shot that crashed like thunder against his ears. A train of flame passed across his temple and powder stung his nostrils. Beauty rolled against him. Another shot rocked the shadows. After this a kind of calm settled down, broken by a long, hiccoughing sigh. Nig Chatto's feet continued to tramp back and forth on the far side of the room.

"Light the light," Beauty mumbled. "I got him."

One more explosion set the furniture to rattling. A match flared for a moment and veered fitfully. By its light, Nig saw a man lying quiet on the floor, blood streaming out of a temple.

CHAPTER 10

THE MOB

Times were indeed getting dangerous. James J. Lestrade had decided as much the night before and he was a great deal more convinced of the fact as he rode rapidly down the Snake River Road toward the Henry place. The day was blistering hot and the heat fog rose like a cloud of steam from the desert. Ordinarily he would have traveled at an easier gait, but the events of the past twenty-four hours pushed him along in spite of himself. In fact, Lestrade was thinking of his own skin and preparing to depart from the country as soon as he could.

His last shipment of beef stock had left his ranges practically bare and throughout the preceding month he had at intervals dropped men from his payroll, stored his ranch accessories, and with a great deal of secrecy stripped his house of its furnishings and sent them on to Portland. All this had been a matter of foresight, for he knew well enough that if the temper of the valley home-steaders ever came to a boil, his own safety would be a matter of doubts. Such work as lay before him could be done from a central office in Portland, while hired agents of his dummy corporation executed the unpleasant details in the region. At some future date—a year or two removed—he knew that most of the settlers would be gone from the scene, discouraged and bankrupt, and he might come back to supervise his holdings. Until that day he was well content to live a town life.

So thinking, he approached the Henry ranch, both pleased and displeased with the result of the last week's accomplishment. Being a careful man, he had struck away from Powder by a trail across the desert that had not touched the Snake River Road until it came within a half mile of his destination. Even so, he did not entirely miss the traffic flowing unevenly along the road. In the short space of the half mile he passed two horsemen and a wagon well loaded with homesteaders.

The very looks of them were disturbing and their curt greetings were more so. The members of the wagon stopped him and began a sharp catechism of the project's affairs which he staved off with the genial assurance that he was in a great deal of a hurry and would be back in town to meet them before noon. Up until that moment he had not been unduly oppressed by the weather, but as he entered the Henry home lot a profuse sweat began to appear on his chubby face.

As usual, Gracie was stirring about in the open, with

the judge nowhere in sight. Lestrade slid from the saddle.

"You look as handsome as a picture, Gracie," he said, essaying to twist the compliment into something more personal.

His fat hand went out to rest on her shoulder, a move that the girl instantly checked by stepping aside. Whatever trust Gracie might have had in Lestrade, it was sadly dissipated now. His demeanor toward her in the intervening week had savored of the unpleasant. Without actually affording her the least discourtesy, he had filled her with repugnance. Now, under the pitiless sun, his face reminded her of an oily ball. He swabbed the moisture from his jowls and puckered his lips into remonstrance.

"Gracie, seems like you don't care much about me anymore. Why, I'm the best friend your father's got."

"I am glad to hear it," the girl said without warmth. "If you want to see Dad, you'll find him in the office."

"There's a lot of things said about me," he proceeded, studying her with his shrewd eyes, "which oughtn't to be listened to by folks like you. These settlers are a grumbling lot. No matter how much a man might do, they'd complain. A grumbling lot."

"I never believe in gossip and I never repeat it," she said. The sight of Lestrade's horse moved her to sympathy. Going over, she led the animal to the shade. "But I am able to judge people fairly well by myself. I find that you can usually tell a man's character by the way he treats his horse."

The shot went home. Lestrade's pink cheeks deepened in color. "Don't let woman's sentiment trouble you so much," he advised a little sharply. "A horse is a horse— nothing more."

"Many men think so," she replied. "I don't."

He let that pass, coming closer to her. "Gracie, I'm

114

here to make an offer. It's plumb unfortunate about the way all our plans went haywire. I'd do 'most anything in my power to right them. But with all that money gone I'm afraid we're busted. It'll mean a loss for most folks and I guess your dad's pretty well tied up like the rest. Now, Gracie, I'd be humbly proud to take that load off him. He's old and he can't fight up the hill like maybe he once could. I've got some money and it'd certainly please me to help."

"Can't you help the rest of the settlers?"

"Lord love you, no. I ain't responsible for them. It's no fault of mine the project is about to go bust. But I can help your dad if—"

"We want no help that others won't get," she said flatly. "We will all share alike."

"Well, I admire that spunk. But think of the old man, Gracie. Just let me take that load from him. Now, I'm not a young man, but I can give you plenty of fine clothes and I can guarantee you a good home—"

He never finished his oblique proposal of marriage. Gracie had been watching him as he spoke. He was an uncomfortably hot and physically unfit specimen as he stood there in the sun, and suddenly she burst into laughter.

"Mr. Lestrade are you asking me to be your wife? Oh, I *must* tell this to Dad!"

He dropped his attempt at sentiment. One big arm swept out and caught her by the wrist, closing around it until she flung up her head in pain.

"Stop that, you little fool!" he cried. "I'll not have anybody laughing at Jim Lestrade! You think you're so high and mighty, eh? Say, I'll bust you and your old man and leave you out on the road, paupers! You be nice to me, girl."

"Let go of my arm!" Her free hand lashed out and struck Lestrade squarely across the mouth.

The man dropped his arm like a shot and rubbed his lips. A slaty hardness came to his eyes.

"You'll suffer for that, girl."

The screen door of the house creaked, and when Lestrade raised his face he saw Judge Henry standing on the steps, a shotgun leveled on him. The judge was in carpet slippers, a figure shaken as if by palsy and with features the color of putty.

"Mr. Lestrade, I saw you take hold of my daughter. You lay your dirty hands on her again, and I shall kill you. I thought you were a gentleman—but now, get out of my yard!"

Lestrade made an attempt to compose himself. "I was telling Gracie," he offered, "that the valley folks are getting pretty well steamed up. I can't guarantee your safety, Judge. Better collect your things and come off with me. I'm bound for the city—"

"Then you're leaving us all to take the loss?" Gracie demanded. "Do you admit you're dishonest? If you had a clear conscience, you'd not be afraid to face them."

"Afraid?" Lestrade blustered. "I ain't afraid. But I've got business in town. As for them homesteaders, they can cry over spilt milk as long as they want. It's no concern of mine. Better get yourself and your daughter fixed up and come along."

For all his vanity and puffiness, the judge was sound at heart. "I stay right here," he said. "I've done right as I saw it to be done. If they want to see me I'll be here on this porch. Gracie you come here. Mr. Lestrade, I bid you good day. You've caused us all trouble. I don't say you're not honest, but I can have nothing more to do with a man who is not a gentleman. Get out of my yard!"

Lestrade swept them both with a long, ugly glare.

"Then stay here and rot," he said, and went to his horse.

He got into the saddle, sawed at the reins and galloped away. Going back down the Snake River Road, he fought to regain composure.

I'm better off without a wife and a doddering father-in-law, he told himself. If they're so blessed stiff-necked they can suffer for it.

A mile from Powder, he left the road and cut across the open ground to enter the town on the far side. He meant to slip quietly through the back door of his office, pick up his papers and his bag and just as quietly leave again. The Orange Ball Limited passed the Junction within the hour, and on that train he aimed to make his departure from the troublous valley.

As he skirted the back of the buildings, he heard a rumbling of men's voices in such proportion that the first flash of alarm ran through him. And when he passed across the rear of a small alley he was astonished to see the size of the crowd milling through the streets. For a moment he debated whether or not it would be best to abandon his trip to the office and go straight to the Junction. But he had come this far and a small portion of pride forbade his scuttling away without his personal effects. So he reached the back of his place and stepped in. What he saw brought a distinct shock.

Confronting him was the man he cared least about seeing at that time—W. W. Offut. The cattleman's face was extremely sober. He came to the point without waste of words.

"You'll please accompany me to the courthouse, Jim."

"What for?" Lestrade said, prepared to argue. "I've got a lot of business on the ranch. Let's wait—"

"Come along," Offut said.

Lestrade's hands shuffled the papers on his desk while his mind shuffled a number of other things. In the end he nodded with the best grace possible.

"All right. What's the trouble?"

"We're having a meeting," Offut said. He followed Lestrade into the street and turned toward the court-house.

The street was crammed and they had not gone a dozen yards before the foremost of the homesteaders spied Lestrade and began to move toward him. At this, Offut pulled back his coat to display his revolver belt and waded serenely through the vanguard. Lestrade comprehended the meaning of this and he felt the blood drain from his face. He began to hear a running fire of comment, all of which he ignored or tossed aside with a brief, "All right, boys, I'll be out to talk this over in a minute."

Offut shoved him inside the courthouse and led him down to the swinging doors that cloaked the judge's chambers. When these swung back James J. Lestrade stopped dead in his tracks and trembled from head to foot.

It was a strange, grim scene. Ranked around the room were most of the big cattlemen of the country, the members of the dreaded committee, and a dozen of W. W. Offut's ranch hands. Seated on one of the benches he found Nig Chatto, a tight-lipped figure who shot him a stony, bitter glance. Beside him was one of his own men, the shifty-eyed Tracy. And beyond Tracy stood Lin Ballou, somewhat pale and with a bandanna wrapped around one wrist.

Lestrade's attention darted from one corner of the chamber to another, and then his interest settled on the clerk's desk. He saw a man stretched full length on the desk, partly covered by a blanket. Lestrade saw the man's wool socks point rigidly toward the ceiling and then he grew cold all over as he recognized the face of Beauty Chatto staring, sightless and indifferent, into space.

Offut was speaking in a slow, solemn manner. "Here he is, boys. I guess we'd better put him upstairs in the cell and keep a good guard. The men outside are in a pretty high state of mind."

"I move," said another, "that we send a messenger after the judge, the prosecuting attorney and the sheriff. They've got no call to be roaming wild with this case unsettled."

"A good idea," Offut approved. "I'll have a man out this very hour."

Then Lestrade recovered from his speechlessness. He said angrily, "You've railroaded a lot of men in this country to suit your politics, but you'll not railroad me. What's all this about?"

The crowd remained silent, waiting for Offut to speak. The cattleman explained it in a few words. "Lin Ballou's been the agent of this committee for several months, trying to run down the unknown parties interested in cattle rustling. He finally connected with the Chattos. Last night he went to bring them back and had a fight in which he killed Beauty. Nig, here, has confessed under promise of leniency. Your foreman, Tracy, volunteered a great deal of information under the same promise. All things told, Jim, you are in for a long, long term of penitentiary life. Sorry. Thought you were a good neighbor."

Tracy stood up and pointed his long finger. He was a man absolutely without loyalty. Having seen how the current of opinion flowed, he had deserted his chief to procure safety for himself. Now he had something else to say.

"I got one more word, folks. Last night when all this

gunplay was going on I had myself hid on the main street near Dan Rounds'. It was Jim Lestrade killed Dan. I saw it with my own eyes."

"You're a liar!" Lestrade yelled. "You're an ex-convict and your word ain't worth a penny!"

All eyes were turned on Tracy. Lestrade saw his chance. He jerked out his gun and threw his body forward. W. W. Offut's great arm fell like an axe across Lestrade's elbow. There was an explosion. A harmless shot tipped up the courtroom floor. Lestrade struggled like a wild man, suddenly surrounded by half a dozen ranch hands.

The shot evoked a sudden answer from the street. The courthouse trembled under a deluge of feet and the swinging doors flew open to let in a stream of settlers. Lin Ballou, running forward, saw Hank Colqueen—patient, hard-working Colqueen—in the lead. The man had become by force of voice and of circumstances the leader of the infuriated mob. He stood on a bench and waved his arms wildly, bellowing out his threat.

"There's Lestrade! Every word he told us was a lie! Where's that money Steele got away with? Why was all the delay and the fire up at Lake Esprit? Why was Chinamen brought in to take away our bread and butter? Lestrade's a skin-game slicker—a tinhorn gambler. He's sharing that embezzled money, believe me!"

The in-rushing crowd roared approval. Colqueen swung like a dancing dervish. "But if you wait for the law to prove it you'll be old and busted. Let's give 'im a sample of valley justice! Pull him out—him and his whole damn crew!"

They kept surging inward, these settlers, forcing cattlemen and prisoners back until they were jammed against the wall. And still there were others clamoring to enter. Ballou and Offut jumped to the judge's rostrum at the same time. The cattleman raised his hand, speaking in a normal voice. The words were utterly lost, but the settlers saw him and something like quiet came into the room. This man was a symbol of honesty and justice.

"Wait a minute," he said. "Don't you boys do anything that'll be on your consciences afterwards. Nobody ever got anywhere by defeating the law. You are all men of good standing. You represent the future of this valley. Many times I have heard you folks speak harshly of the old days when everything ran wild. Well, you are right. Don't make that error yourselves. Remember, it's you men who will serve on the jury in this man's case or, if not, at least men of your own kind. Fair play! Give the man a chance in court."

"Did he give us a chance?" Colqueen roared. "It was all a passel of lies! Lies from beginning to end. If he was square he wouldn't be there cringing like a whipped dog, nor he wouldn't have tried to get away. But we ain't got no proof of that in a court. He's guilty as Satan—but there's not enough evidence to put him where he belongs. You figure that to be justice?"

"Who said there wasn't evidence?" Offut demanded. "Maybe there's no evidence to hold him on the land deal, but we've got him caught on cattle thievery. This man was a confederate of the Chattos. There's not a judge who wouldn't put him in prison."

The more thoughtful members of the mob began to collect themselves. Ballou, scanning the upturned faces, saw reason coming back. But Colqueen and the younger hot-heads were still smarting under their troubles.

"Who says there's evidence enough?" Colqueen demanded.

Offut put a hand on Ballou's shoulder, at which the hubbub rose again and continued for several minutes.

Until then Lin had never quite realized the sentiment against him. It ran terribly strong. From several corners he was assailed by jeering, half-articulate malice which Colqueen managed to express in words.

"Him? Why, Lin's a cattle rustler himself. You ought to know that, seeing as you caught him. Take his word? Far as us homesteaders are concerned it don't make no difference how many cows are stolen. It's none of our concern. But damn it, we're going to get some satisfaction for losing all our money."

"No—no—no," Offut said, patiently repeating the words until he had command of their attention again.

Ballou's attention switched to another part of the room. The long, angular frame of his companion of the mesa, Bill, towered in the doorway and tried to wedge himself through the packed crowd. He motioned to Lin and nodded his head vigorously several times. Offut, meanwhile, had calmed the mob somewhat.

"You folks are impatient. Lin Ballou is as straight as a string. As honest as I am. I'll vouch for him, and if you know my reputation that must count for something. He has been my agent—the agent of the cattle committee. He had to make himself out a crook to catch other crooks. It is due to him that we've got the Chattos—one dead, one alive—and that we can put Lestrade in prison. You boys owe Lin an apology."

This was a poser. Coming from such a man as W. W. Offut it was not to be lightly challenged. Offut had never in his life been anything but square and they knew it. There and then the animus of the mob seemed to lose its strength, the members of it recollecting their better senses. Lin Ballou stepped down from the rostrum, caught hold of Bill's onward reaching arm and by sheer strength pulled him through the last rank of the crowd.

"Tell me in a hurry. What's the answer? How'd you get back so sudden?"

"I thought I'd better speed things," Bill whispered, "so I dropped off at Pinto and used the telegraph. Got an answer to the effect that we was authorized to just about write our own ticket. Now you get up there and spill it. It'll be happy news for somebody."

Ballou stepped back to the rostrum and faced the waiting crowd. "Let me have a word in this controversy. You folks had better forget Lestrade and let him take what the judge hands him. Which will sure be plenty. I know you folks are out a pile and I can just about tell you why. Lestrade never wanted to finish that irrigation scheme. If he knows as much about the land in this valley as I do —and I think he does—he wanted to get hold of it for himself."

"Heck of a lot of good he'll get from it," Colqueen muttered, for once losing his faith in the land.

"As far as farming goes, that's right," Lin agreed. "You boys who were at the dance that time will remember I bucked like a steer at the idea of water. Why? Because this country can't afford it. But there is something under all this sand and alkali that's worth forty thousand farms."

That caught the crowd's attention. Every last man craned his neck.

"You boys thought I was an awful fool frittering my time away, prospecting for gold. And I would have been a fool, sure enough, if gold was what I wanted. But it wasn't. Bill here—" he motioned to the lanky youth— "is a geologist. The best in this man's state. He's employed by the Alamance Mineral Corporation. Guess you know that name, don't you?"

Very few didn't. It ranked as the largest mining concern in the state. Even W. W. Offut turned his head when he heard the name, and watched Lin closely.

"Well, the sum and substance of it is," Lin went on, enjoying the suspense, "that Bill and I have been all over the valley floor, poking little holes in the ground. That's a sideline nobody knows anything about. As a result I can announce with a right smart amount of satisfaction that this valley is underlaid with what may be the richest bed of potash in America."

There was a sound as if a gust of wind had passed through the room. Hank Colqueen shook his head several times. W. W. Offut began to smile, a rare thing for him.

"Now potash," Lin proceeded, "is a mighty valuable thing. I'm no teacher, but I might say it's so valuable that most of it comes from Europe. Bill tells me to say that the Alamance Mineral Corporation is ready—if all tests are as good as those we have made—to stand back of a development of these beds to the fullest extent. That means we'll prosper. That's all I've got to say, except to point out that this is probably the reason Lestrade wanted to break all you folks and take the land himself."

"Lestrade and Judge Henry—" Colqueen started to break in with a last dying spark of rebellion.

"Judge Henry had nothing to do with it," Lin Ballou said. "Lestrade worked him. You ought to be able to figure that out."

A voice came from the rear of the crowd. Lin saw Judge Henry standing unsteadily in the doorway, one arm holding to his daughter. "Boys, boys, if you think I'm a crook, I'll turn over any profit I make to you. It ain't much, because I'm stuck as deep as the rest, but whatever comes from the Henry place is yours."

The crowd roared—not with resentment this time, but

124

with approval. Those nearest the judge slapped him on the back. Hank Colqueen disappeared in the sea of bobbing faces, no more to be seen. Lin jumped from the rostrum and fought his way through the mass until he was beside Gracie. The girl seemed on the point of crying. Whether it was from happiness or sorrow Lin could not tell, until she looked up to him and smiled, lips trembling.

"Oh, Lin, I'm so glad folks know you're straight—as I've known so very, very long."

"What made you come here?" Lin demanded. "Into all this grief?"

In a few words she told him of Lestrade's visit. "After that," she said, "Dad saw settlers going toward Powder and he decided to face them immediately. You don't know what a strain it's been and how glad I am it's all over."

"I think," he said, growing red, "that I really ought to get a reward."

"What?"

"I think you should go home and bake me another apple pie."

"Oh," she said in a disappointed tone. "Is that all?"

"Well," Lin said, "that will be all until I get you in the kitchen where all these yahoos won't be looking."

And that night as the stars came out and the coyotes sent forth their quivering challenge, Powder settled again into its somnolence, with another chapter added to its brief but vivid history. Out in the bleak graveyard they buried Beauty Chatto and Dan Rounds, side by side, while the jail held three miserable, defeated men—Nig Chatto, James J. Lestrade, and Tracy the turn-coat. They were fit company for one another.

And over in Judge Henry's house, supper was past and

the judge had the ranch to himself. Lin and Grace had driven to that long deserted homestead of Lin's. It seemed Grace wanted to take measurements for new curtains.

YOU WILL WANT TO READ THESE
ACTION-PACKED WESTERNS BY MAX BRAND,
KING OF WESTERN WRITERS!

- [ ] **SILVERTIP'S SEARCH** (64-860, 75¢)
- [ ] **SILVERTIP'S TRAP** (64-859, 75¢)
- [ ] **SILVERTIP'S ROUNDUP** (64-813, 75¢)
- [ ] **THE LONG CHANCE** (64-784, 75¢)
- [ ] **THE MAN FROM MUSTANG** (64-767, 75¢)
- [ ] **MISTRAL** (64-686, 75¢)
- [ ] **DEAD OR ALIVE** (64-708, 75¢)
- [ ] **SMILING CHARLIE** (64-656, 75¢)
- [ ] **PLEASANT JIM** (64-633, 75¢)
- [ ] **THE RANCHER'S REVENGE** (64-611, 75¢)
- [ ] **THE DUDE** (64-582, 75¢)
- [ ] **THE JACKSON TRAIL** (64-541, 75¢)
- [ ] **THE IRON TRAIL** (64-528, 75¢)
- [ ] **PILLAR MOUNTAIN** (64-509, 75¢)

MORE SIX-GUN EXCITEMENT IN
THESE GREAT WESTERNS BY
ERNEST HAYCOX . . .